Mallory Weber is a school counselor and a licensed clinical professional counselor. She lives in Illinois with her husband, Bryce, and her three young daughters: Brynn, Tessa, and Reese.

Mallory loves to read and one of her greatest aspirations was to write a book that inspires someone or is 'worth reading.' She created the story line for *The Beaten Heart* when she was in a very dark time in her life. It gave her purpose, and writing was her therapy. Ten years later, she finally finished it.

Never give up on a dream, no matter what anyone else says. If you can't stop thinking about something, there's a reason.

I dedicate this book to my mom. She showed me that even if I hadn't found my own happily-ever-after, I could write the ending I always wanted. To my girls – never, ever change anything about yourself for a boy. Stay true to yourself and the right person will love you for who you are.

Mallory Weber

THE BEATEN HEART

AUSTIN MACAULEY PUBLISHERS™

LONDON • CAMBRIDGE • NEW YORK • SHARJAH

Ordering Information
Quantity sales: Special discounts are available on quantity purchases by corporations, associations, and others. For details, contact the publisher at the address below.

Publisher's Cataloging-in-Publication data
Weber, Mallory
The Beaten Heart

ISBN 9781645751595 (Paperback)
ISBN 9781645751601 (Hardback)
ISBN 9781645751618 (ePub e-book)

Library of Congress Control Number: 2021913038

www.austinmacauley.com/us

First Published (2021)
Austin Macauley Publishers LLC
40 Wall Street, 33rd Floor, Suite 3302
New York, NY 10005
USA

mail-usa@austinmacauley.com
+1 (646) 5125767

Things don't go wrong and break your heart so you can become bitter and give up. They happen to break you down and build you up so you can be all that you were intended to be.

The Beginning
July 4, 1993

A flash of light shot across the sky followed by a thunderous *BOOM!* The air smelled heavy with smoke and there were popping and cracking sounds. Red, green, blue, and white glittered the night. Suddenly, the whole sky was illuminated by fireworks reflecting off of the lake. Eight-year-olds Melanie and Drake lay sprawled out in the back of Drake's parents' boat. It was July, but a cool night. They were huddled underneath a blanket trying to stay warm. Drake grabbed Melanie's hand and squeezed. He told her to wish on one of the fireworks.

Melanie said, "Silly, you can't wish on fireworks. You wish on stars."

Drake said, "Why can't you wish on fireworks? They are just like bright, colorful shooting stars. Let's just try it."

Melanie agreed saying, "Okay, fine. I will wish on a firework, but I am pretty sure it will not come true." Melanie was the smart one. She read every book she could get her hands on and felt more at ease having intelligent conversations with adults than playing games with children. Drake knew she was probably right and you really couldn't wish on a firework, but it seemed like a good idea.

Suddenly, a stream of red rocketed across the sky. Drake and Melanie closed their eyes and wished aloud. Melanie said, "I hope that we are always friends. You are my best friend and I want you to be my best friend for my whole life."

Drake said, "I will always be your best friend. You are my best friend and you will marry me one day. Oh, and I want to win my baseball game tomorrow."

Just like that, the fireworks show was over as quickly as it began. Melanie and Drake lay on the boat talking until it was time to dock the boat and head home. As Drake held Melanie's hand, she started to think about what happened earlier that day. Melanie was standing terrified on the high dock looking into the looming water below. She grabbed her raft, closed her eyes, and tried to make herself jump into the lake below. When she opened her eyes, she was still standing on the high dock trembling. The water below was filled with kids chanting, "Chicken, scaredy-cat, baby." She knew she was none of those things, but she was scared of heights and not a fan of swimming in the murky, brown lake. The idea of swimming where she couldn't see what was under her feet wasn't appealing to her. Not to mention the fact that there were lots and lots of fish and even worse, snakes! Melanie hated snakes! Suddenly, her best friend Drake was climbing up the ladder behind her.

He grabbed her hand and said, "Don't be scared. I will jump with you and nothing bad will ever happen to you." Instantly, she was not afraid anymore. She squeezed his hand, gripped her raft, and jumped. She landed in the water with a splash.

She thought to herself, *That wasn't so bad.* It was amazing how safe she felt when Drake was around. He really was her best friend and she knew that he would never let anything bad ever happen to her.

As she lay on the boat against her best friend, she thought how lucky she was to have a friend like Drake. He stuck up for her when other kids were teasing her about not jumping into the lake. He was always there when she needed him. She realized that her wish was silly and that they would always be best friends even without wishing on fireworks.

Chapter 1

2014

She stood on her tip toes, her 5'8" frame just not tall enough to reach the top shelf without assistance. Her fingertips grazed the edge of a box. The desired suitcase was within reach. She just needed to move that box a few inches. She could feel the cardboard starting to slip. She jumped and hit the box again.

A stocking cap fell and landed on top of her head. She shook her ponytail as her brown hair went flying. She laughed thinking to herself, *I don't need that here in Florida.*

She jumped and hit the box for a second time. A beach bag, contents spewing, fell instead. She was pelted with a bottle of sunscreen.

Third time is the charm, she thought as she jumped again. Finally, the suitcase came loose. As she lifted the heavy plastic suitcase over her head, a box toppled down as well. Moving to Florida, she did not take the time to unpack or sort through any of her boxes from college. She never meant for this box to make the move. Surprised, she started to pick up the contents and was surrounded by familiar faces of her hometown friends, pictures from grade school and high school. It was funny to look at how much they had grown up and changed. As she sifted through the items, memories flooded her mind.

Something shiny caught her eye. Purple, blue, green, and gold; the way the colors rippled almost looked like it was made of glitter. She held the shiny rock in her hand as she remembered the day, vividly.

March 1996

Ten-year-old Melanie stood in awe, surrounded by so many options. The lights in the gift shop made the rocks glisten and sparkle. She knew what she wanted to spend her allowance money on the instant they walked in the door.

She needed rocks for her rock collection, but not just any rocks from her yard would do. She had been gifted several unique ones for Christmas earlier this year, but she still wanted more. The Field Museum was the perfect place to add such treasures to her growing collection.

Her best friend Drake ran around the store, scooping up rocks and trying to help her decide.

He shouted, "What about pyrite? Do you have that one?"

"Already got it."

"Hmm, quartz?"

"Nope, got that one too."

"How about peacock ore? That looks like something you would like."

"Peacock ore? No, I don't have that one. Should I get it?"

"It looks pretty cool. Here, what do you think?"

"Whoa, that is super neat. It looks like it's magical."

"Yeah, it does. It's like a rainbow."

"Oh, but wait, check these out!"

"Umm, they just look like boring rocks."

"That's what they want you to think. Read the sign, they are geodes. You break them open and then look what is inside."

"Okay, that is super cool!"

"I know, but I still like the peacock ore too. Ugh… I can't decide. I think I only have enough money for one."

"Then get the geodes. We can break them open together and each have one half."

"That's a good point."

As their moms helped Melanie choose the geodes, she did not notice Drake sneak away to buy the peacock ore.

Melanie excitedly thought to herself as she unzipped her Hello Kitty coin purse, *it was just supposed to be a normal Saturday. Nothing out of the ordinary. I planned on watching cartoons and playing Barbies with my little sister Madison.*

When Drake's mom, Veronica, called late last night, she had no idea this was what their parents had planned. Drake's dad had an important meeting in the city. They were taking the company plane for the day. Veronica told Drake he could invite one friend to come along. Drake picked Melanie out of all of his friends.

Melanie carefully unfolded her wrinkled dollars as she counted the exact amount for one large geode. She couldn't wait to break the dull, gray rock and see the beauty inside.

The flight there was pretty smooth, even though Melanie was not a big fan of flying. She gripped the armrest, her hot pink glitter fingernails digging into the cold metal.

Drake tried to distract her by playing "I spy" and asking questions from her "Brain Quest" cards. She loved all kinds of trivia games and the two of them excitedly quizzed each other. The games eventually worked. When she looked out the window, they were safely on the ground.

Exploring the exhibits, learning about mummies, examining fossils; her mind had been preoccupied, but still she had been dreading the return flight all day.

As they prepared for takeoff, her best friend Drake grabbed her hand. Her fingers clasped around something cold and metallic feeling. As she opened her hand, she saw a stream of glittering, bright colors.

The peacock ore I wanted! she thought to herself.

She thanked her friend Drake and knew their friendship was special. They would always be best friends.

Chapter 2
2014

As she examined the contents of the box; postcards from years at summer camp, concert tickets, movie stubs, a birthday crown. So many memories; so many moments she had forgotten. She was flooded with emotions, both happy and sad. Some of her friendships no longer existed. A ripped, faded piece of notebook paper was folded so many times it resembled some form of Japanese origami.

She unfolded the edges and tried to flatten it so the contents were legible. She could make out squiggly, childhood handwriting. She laughed as she realized it was a letter Drake had sent from camp. They were "Pen Pals" every year as they both went to different camps, but during the same time, the letters barely made it to camp before one of them returned home. Still, it was a tradition they shared.

Aug. 4, 1996

Mel,

Baseball camp is awesome.
I am learning to pitch super-fast. I hit a homerun yesterday and we get new bats and gloves.

Hope you're having fun. Are you swimming in the lake?

See you next week!

Drake

She put the contents back in the box. She thought to herself, *I need more time to sort through this. There are way too many memories.*

She left the box where it sat on her bedroom floor as she hurriedly tried to fix her shoulder-length, brown hair. She hastily applied mascara and tried to look like she wasn't as stressed as she felt. She planned to surprise her boyfriend, Clayton, by cooking dinner tonight.

She was tired from studying all day. She desperately needed to pack, but still she wanted to make her boyfriend dinner. She had been dating Clayton for almost two years and everything was going pretty well. Although, she just didn't feel the butterflies and magic that the movies all talked about.

Clayton was from her home state of Illinois and she had known him for several years. He was a great guy, but she just wasn't in love with him.

She knew it and she was pretty sure he felt the same way, but even so, they were still together. He was too nice for her to break up with him. She was planning on making him a surprise dinner because she was heading home for her close friend's wedding that weekend.

Normally, she would invite Clayton to be her date, but since he had just opened his own physical therapy clinic, he just didn't have the time to take off for the weekend. She pretended to be sad, but in actuality she was sort of relieved.

Her friend Katherine (Kate) was marrying Daniel, one of her closest childhood friends and she didn't feel like entertaining an "outsider." She remembered how crazy she had felt when Kate had called her last winter and told her the news.

She did not want to drag Clayton along when she didn't even know how she felt about this event. It wasn't like she was in love with Kate's fiancée, no, quite the opposite actually; she was pretty sure she still had feelings for Daniel's brother, Drake, even though she knew she shouldn't.

Drake was the one boy she knew she had let "get away." He had been her best friend growing up and they were practically inseparable.

When Melanie looked back on her childhood, there were very few moments Drake was not a part of. Melanie never missed one of his baseball games, he was a staple at her family events, and their families even went on trips together. She could remember being the only girl at all of his birthday parties and how special he always made her feel. Somehow everything changed. It's not like they stopped being friends. When Melanie thought about it, she didn't really remember what had happened.

In high school they still hung out and he would always greet her with a huge hug if they ran into each other at a party. When she went away to college, Drake was constantly asking her to visit, but she always turned him down. The last time he invited her, she had chosen to visit her friend Ryan that weekend instead.

Drake and Daniel Jameson were like her brothers growing up. She had not seen him in four years and was pretty uneasy about how things were going to be during the wedding weekend.

Of course, Kate and Daniel had made him best man and she was a bridesmaid. Since the wedding was in the city almost four hours from her hometown, she knew they would be seeing a lot of each other over the weekend. She tried to act like nothing was bothering her as she pulled into the parking lot of the condominium complex.

Chopping garlic; drizzling olive oil; the pan was sizzling on the stove. The savory aroma filled the air of the apartment. She heard a knock at the door. Clayton's friendly smile greeted her as he enveloped her in a hug. He looked tired, but happy. She knew the new practice was taking most of his time and energy and she was happy to do something nice for him.

As he entered her apartment, he sniffed the air. He winked one brown eye at her saying, "Hey good lookin', what ya got cookin'?"

She laughed, "It's a surprise. Why don't you just relax while I handle dinner."

He opened a bottle of wine and she got right to work in the kitchen.

She knew she should be happy with the way her life was going after all she had been through, but she just didn't feel like she thought she should. Her mother was always joking with her, saying that her love of Lifetime Movie Network had her living in a dream world.

She'd say, "Mel, real life isn't always like a fairy tale. Sometimes you just find someone who loves you and treats you right and you make a great life together. It's not always rainbows and butterflies."

Melanie sipped her glass of wine as she cut tomatoes, peeled garlic, and sautéed the shrimp. Clayton kept offering to help so she had him broil some garlic bread and make salad. He told her all about his day at the clinic. He had a new patient, a star basketball player that had recently blown his ACL and was in an intensive program to be back in time for the fall semester. Apparently, he had loads of potential and scouts from all over Florida were interested in him as long as he could play next season. So, Clayton had his work cut out for him.

She loved watching him talk about his job, he seemed so passionate and so sure of himself. He asked how her day was and she told him all about studying and the new malpractice suit at the firm she worked at. She was only a legal assistant for now, but as soon as she passed the bar exam, they said she would be a member of the firm. So, her days were spent studying for the bar and working part time. She had graduated four months ago and was supposed to be taking the bar exam in February. Five months may seem like a long time away, but she knew the test date would be here sooner than she hoped. She studied day and night.

Although, she was almost 28 and most of her classmates were only 25, she was happy with her decision to go back to school.

After graduating almost six years ago from undergrad, she searched for a job in the advertising world only to be extremely disappointed. The economy at that time was terrible and unemployment was at one of its all-time highs. After being unemployed and bored out of her mind for almost a year, she decided to go back to school. She had said she wanted an adventure after graduating, so she only applied to out-of-state law schools where it was much warmer than the Illinois climate she was used to. It was one of the best decisions she had ever made and she actually felt like she was doing something for the first time in years. Melanie did not have a typical college experience, but it wasn't due to her home life, or a hardship she faced, it was because she had followed her heart and not her mind.

Originally, she went to a private out-of-state school for her undergraduate degree in advertising, but after the second semester of her junior year, she had transferred to a nearby state school to be closer to her then boyfriend, Ryan. She had dated Ryan for almost four years and after the second year she had decided the long distance was just too much to deal with.

First, she thought the move was the greatest thing that had ever happened and as both of their graduations grew near, the talk of marriage had gone from a dream to a reality. They had looked at rings, had their dream house built in their minds, and he had told her that by the next fall they would be engaged. It seemed like she was going to get the happily ever after just like in the movies, except her dream quickly changed into a nightmare instead.

Ryan was extremely smart, but he only wanted to go to one school, Duke. Melanie believed in him and had no doubt that he would surely be accepted. They visited Durham and fell in love with everything about it. So, Ryan and Melanie had put all their hopes and dreams into the plan that she would move in with him and find a job near where he went to school. She was so happy with the idea of having a plan and just focused on graduating. They never even thought about what would happen if he wasn't accepted.

She will never forget the day that the letter came, only it was not the good news they had both been expecting.

Melanie finished her class and went to Ryan's apartment. She saw the mail sitting on his desk. She knew better than to ask if he had heard anything from Duke.

"Hey babe, you want to go to the bar? Couple guys from class are up there."

"What? Why would I want to go to the bar? It is 2:00 in the afternoon. You should be studying. Finals are next week. We graduate in two weeks! How can you even think of drinking right now?"

"You seriously sound like my mom. You need to chill. I can drink if I want to."

She was able to talk him into just watching a movie, but she knew something felt off. She decided to forgo studying and stay the night with him. As the night went on, he didn't mention anything about Duke. He acted fine during the movie, like nothing was wrong. It was only right before having sex, in between kissing, he had looked at her with his sad, green eyes.

"Do you really love me?"

Confused, she answered, "Yes, of course. You know this. Why are you asking? Why else would I be here with you? Staying the night when I should be at my place, studying."

She couldn't understand why he was ruining this moment with a silly question like that when he obviously knew the answer. Why else would she be in his bed, in his arms, if she didn't really love him. He hugged her tighter than ever and she thought about how safe she felt in between those big, strong arms and nestled her head into the crook of his shoulder. He kissed her neck.

He whispered in her ear, "I am so happy because I did not get into Duke and I do not know what I would do without you."

She hugged him back and reassured him that everything would be fine.

"We'll figure out a different plan. We can still move to North Carolina if you want. Let's just look for jobs instead."

He seemed okay with her answer and they had fallen asleep next to each other.

Everything seemed to be okay for a week or so. Except he seemed to be angrier. The littlest things would set him off. He started withdrawing more and more.

The next week, she was in the communications lab working on a group project and was surprised that he was calling her in the middle of the afternoon. She knew he was supposed to be in class taking a quiz. She could hear the slurring in his voice and knew something wasn't right.

"Babe, come to the bar. It's fun. Mike is buying shots."

"Sorry. I am busy studying. Why aren't you in class?"

"I blew it off. It's not like I won't graduate. Who cares what my grades are now? As long as I pass, I can still graduate. Come on, let's have fun."

She hung up the phone and knew he was not okay. *I know his rejection letter is really bothering him. I just wish he would talk to me about it. Drinking instead of taking a quiz. What is he thinking?*

She spent the rest of the week studying and ignored him mostly. *I care about my grades. Besides his drinking is getting annoying. I always have to be the responsible one.*

She could never have a good time because she had to make sure he wasn't going to do anything crazy. After she took her last exam, she wanted to celebrate. It also happened to be Cinco de Mayo, so a lot of the college kids were out drinking anyway. She went to meet her friend Lilly for some martinis. Lilly used to date one of Ryan's roommates, Garrett. She was still friends with the boys even after they broke up.

After ordering her second "Flirtini," Melanie glanced up to see Ryan and his friend Jake in the doorway of the bar. He quickly ran over and gave her a quick kiss on the cheek and asked how her final went. She was kind of upset that he had interrupted her girls' night, but Lilly being friends with the boys too, said it was fine.

"It will be fun."

"Sure you don't care?"

"Nope. We will have fun no matter what."

The four left the martini bar and headed to get some Coronas in honor of the holiday. Everything was going well and everyone seemed to be having a great time. Then Jake decided it was time for a smoke break.

Ryan followed and when they came back 20 minutes later, it was obvious that something was not right.

Lilly pointed it out first saying, "Ryan, what happened to you? How are you so messed up? You were fine 20 minutes ago?"

Ryan just looked at both girls and smiled and laughed saying, "Oh, I am not that bad, we are just having a good time."

Melanie ran into a girl she had three classes. She knew it was her birthday, so she bought her a drink. She never noticed Ryan was right behind her.

After the girl had gulped her shot and rejoined her birthday celebration, Ryan laid into Melanie.

"Oh, so now I see how you really are, Melanie, thanks for introducing me! Since I am not going to be a doctor, I am not good enough to meet your friends anymore! Who the hell do you think you are?"

Not wanting to cause a scene, Melanie pulled Ryan to the side.

"I didn't even know you were behind me. How could I introduce someone I didn't even know was there?"

She could tell that trying to be logical was pointless. He was clearly too messed up to see her side of the story. Expecting to see familiar love and understanding, she was scared to see the familiar warm, green eyes were replaced with an evil, cold look. She knew in her heart that something was not right.

"Look, I don't want to fight. Tonight was supposed to be fun for me for once. I have been studying for weeks. I am graduating too. I just wanted to have some fun with my friends. I am going to go home and I'll talk to you in the morning."

She tried to hug him goodbye, but he just walked off. She told Lilly she was leaving. She drove back to her apartment, annoyed that the night was ruined and desperately needing sleep. She sent Ryan a good night text and locked her door.

Since her roommate Savannah had moved out earlier than expected, her once warm, comfortable apartment was now lonely and eerily quiet. Savannah had recently gotten a full-time job and had moved into a townhouse 20 minutes away. She lay in bed thinking, *I'm so glad I am graduating in four days. Everything is going to be okay. Ryan and I will make a new plan. It's all going to be okay.*

She woke up at 3:35 am to Ryan standing over her bed. Giving him a key seemed like a really stupid idea, especially when he was in a mood like tonight. She almost forgot she had given him a key. Her first instinct was to scream.

Her screams just made him mad. He jumped on the bed and pushed her face into her pillow trying to muffle her screams. She was kicking and trying to push him away. He kept hitting her over and over. Hitting her in the back of the head. Grabbing her by the neck and trying to choke her. She kept fighting back.

If I could just make him stop. I wish I could reach the baseball bat behind my bed. If I grab it though, it's going to be worse. He's bigger and stronger than me. What if he used the bat on me instead? Maybe I could get a knife out of the kitchen.

Ryan held her hands against her body, so tight that she couldn't move. She was completely powerless. Losing faith and giving up any chance of getting out of his grip, she started praying silently in her mind.

Please, God, just save me. Let me live to see the sunrise. Let me graduate and make a new life. I won't go back to Ryan. Just please help me.

Finally, she felt his grip loosen and she was able to move her hands. Thinking it was over she started yelling at him, asking him what he was doing and why he was here. He never answered her, just started punching her again and shoving her head into the headboard.

After what felt like hours he stopped and pulled himself on top of her, which is where he passed out. She lay there all night unable to move, only talking to God in her head and pleading for someone to help her. When he finally rolled off of her, she still lay frozen, unsure of what to do.

Should she leave? Where would she go? If she left now, he would surely find her. What if he woke up even angrier? How did she even get herself into this situation?

She just laid there waiting for the right time to try and sneak away.

He started to move. She mentally tried to prepare herself for more blows to the head. Closing her eyes, ready for the next punch.

"Good morning! Do you want pancakes or waffles for breakfast?"

Dumbfounded, she was shocked.

How could someone be such a monster one minute and offer her breakfast the next?

She jumped out of bed screaming at him, telling him what he had done just a few hours ago.

"You are crazy. You broke into my place and started hitting me for no reason. I mean like really hitting me. Choking me, suffocating me. I thought you were going to kill me."

He did not believe her and clearly had no memory of what just happened.

"I think you just had a bad dream. You're obviously really upset though, so I am just going to go."

She couldn't believe how he was acting. She didn't know what to do. She took a shower and just sat on the shower floor sobbing.

Who does that to someone they supposedly love?

She knew she needed to go home. She refused to take his calls. She turned her phone off. The entire drive home she went over and over the events in her mind.

Should she tell someone? Should she call the police? Should she tell her mom? Her friends? What should she do? Was this a one-time thing? What the hell just happened?

She knew what had happened was real. She didn't just have a bad dream. She also knew deep down that it wasn't a one-time thing.

He's never hurt me like this, but his drinking has been a problem for a while. Seriously every time he drinks, we fight.

Arguing was one thing, but what happened last night was completely against everything she believed. He just wouldn't give up. When she finally turned her phone back on, her voicemail was flooded with "I'm sorry messages."

"Babe, I am sorry. I don't know what happened. I am really, really sorry. Just talk to me. Come back here and let's be together."

She kept driving and thinking. The image of his angry, green eyes, as his fists hit her. His fingers closing around her throat made her feel sick. In the past, she forgave him. His apologies and most likely flowers helped her forget the fighting. Not this time—hearing his voicemails, his voice repulsed her. She threw her phone at the empty passenger seat.

I can't go back to him. I just can't. Even if he's sorry. What if it happens again?

She knew he would say, "he couldn't remember" and most likely that she was "overreacting." As she pulled into her childhood home, she put a brave face on. Plastered a fake smile on her face and told her parents she just needed to go home for a few days.

Her thoughts were interrupted by the timer buzzing and she looked up from the stove to see Clayton setting the table and carrying their wine glasses to the table. She blinked, trying to erase the thoughts from her mind and began serving the pasta onto plates.

Chapter 3

2014

The dinner was great and Clayton praised her cooking.

"You can seriously cook. This was some gourmet cuisine."

She smiled thinking how kind he was, *If only I could make myself love him the way I should.*

He pretended not to mind when she picked their billionth chick flick only wanting to please her.

When the movie was over, he looked at the clock.

"Mel, it's getting late. I should probably go. You know you have a plane to catch tomorrow."

Clayton knew she had trust issues and respected her decision not to stay together even if they were nearing 30. Clayton was a cousin to the husband of one of her best friends. They had met at their wedding and had stayed friends. It was only after she had started law school in Florida that they realized they were living in the same city and should meet up.

One date turned into a weekly dinner or movie and now here they were.

He was so kind and understanding. Even when she explained about Ryan.

"I just haven't seriously dated anyone since my ex."

He understood how hard it was for her to trust someone. It had taken Melanie more than two years to get over Ryan and move past what had happened. Even when she was over him, she still wasn't okay being in a relationship with someone.

The thoughts of what happened with Ryan haunted her mind. She tried to bring herself back to the present, but she was always reminded.

The night she unexpectedly returned home from college, Melanie sat through family dinner. If her parents knew anything was wrong, they didn't act like it. No one asked her how she was or mentioned Ryan.

Desperate to get out of the house and away from her thoughts, she met her friend Sydney.

Melanie held it together as Sydney filled her in on her life. Melanie listened and asked questions as Sydney told her all about her accounting internship and the new job she accepted. She would be moving in August and she was excited for her friend. Her happiness for Sydney was genuine, but when the subject of Ryan was brought up, the facade started to crumble.

"So, how's Ryan? Are you two moving away together after graduation? What's your plan?"

Melanie could barely contain her sobs. She broke down telling Sydney what had happened just the night before. The look on her face told Melanie that this was not right.

"You cannot go back to him. You need to go to the police. I can't believe he did that. I am just so glad you're okay."

Sydney hugged her with tears in her eyes. Melanie knew she shouldn't forgive him.

I just can't picture my life without him. Four years is a long time.

She couldn't imagine her life without him. They had built a life together, sharing friends, and practically living together.

Melanie stayed in her hometown until the morning of her graduation. She refused to take Ryan's calls, thanks in a large part to Sydney.

"You can't talk to him. If you do. I will tell your parents what you told me."

She kept her promise. It wasn't easy though, Ryan kept calling. She had so many missed calls and voicemails that she went to Verizon and had his number blocked.

She thought, *Now, he can call me, but I won't even know he tried.*

He was sneaky though and would find other ways to contact her. He emailed her.

He called and texted her from other people's phones.

"Melanie, you need to tell that boy to leave you alone and he better never call me asking for you again."

Melanie's dad had been furious when Ryan called him begging her to talk to him. Ryan didn't know Melanie's parents knew what happened.

Melanie never told them. Sydney kept her promise, but Madison overheard the two girls talking on the phone. Worried about her big sister's safety, she confided in her parents.

Melanie was embarrassed to admit she had even found herself in such a bad situation.

Her mom just sat there listening with tears in her eyes.

"Melanie, I told you he wasn't right for you. He didn't make you happy. I just never knew he was so awful to you. Promise me, you will never see him again."

"I promise, Mom. I know."

Her mom hugged her, "If there's anything you need, dad and I will help you."

Melanie hugged her mom, thankful for their support.

"There's just one small thing, though Mel. You're going to have to pack up your apartment. Dad and I can help if you want us too."

"I can do it Mom. I'm a big girl. Savannah needs to get some more of her stuff anyway. I'll talk to her and plan a time next week."

Melanie and Savannah spent the day packing up the apartment. Thankfully, Savannah took most of the furniture. Melanie just needed to get her clothes and pretty much everything could fit in her car. Taking her picture frames off the walls, packing up her memories, tears streamed down her face.

This was not how I pictured moving out of this place.

No longer excited about the future, she knew she needed a new plan. The girls carried the last box to the car and hugged each other goodbye. It was getting dark and Melanie knew she needed to just go home. For some reason, she couldn't just leave town. Being there, surrounded by their memories, she realized she needed closure. Ryan still had a few of her things. Sure, she could go on without them, but a small part of her wanted to see him one last time. She needed to see if she really was over him.

Driving to his place she thought…

I am just going to tell him I am really finished. I am going to get my things and then I am going to move on with my life.

He was standing outside as she pulled into the parking lot. She took it as a sign that they needed to talk face to face. He listened as she explained she was done, but when she tried to leave, he grabbed her.

"Babe, please, I am sorry. I love you. I don't want to be with anyone else. I don't want to live without you. You're my life. You make my life whole."

"I know. You were my whole life too. I'll think about working things out."

She told him, "I'll think about giving us another chance."

She wasn't being honest though. She could never forgive him for what he did.

Who does that to someone they supposedly love?

He had apologized profusely saying, "I admit it. I was sad about not getting into Duke. I did some coke. That's why I don't remember what happened at your apartment. It messed me up really bad and I blacked out. I'll never use it again."

Listening to his apologies in person, *I can't believe it.*

He didn't even own up to what he did. He blamed everything on drugs.

She didn't care what his excuse was.

Maybe it was the drugs, but either way, he scared me more than I've ever been scared.

Later that night, at home in her room, she wrote him a goodbye email.

I hope someday we can be friends, but right now I am not ready to forgive you. I am sorry for what happened, but I am not ready to move past it.

Reading her email, she realized she actually said she was partly sorry for what happened. She couldn't believe she was apologizing for him attacking her. She knew that getting back together with him would be the biggest mistake of her life. She hit send and prayed that he wouldn't do anything too crazy.

She woke up to her phone ringing at 4 am. Confused and unaware of the time, she answered. She could barely make out what the person was saying. Looking back, she just thought Lilly was drinking and drunk dialing her, but deep down she knew something was wrong.

"Lilly, what's going on? Are you okay?"

"Mel, Garrett just called me. Ryan got in an accident."

"Is he okay?"

She could hear Lilly take a deep breath and choke back a sob.

"Mel, he didn't make it. He's dead. I'm so sorry."

Lilly didn't know what Ryan had done. She didn't know Melanie had broken things off for good.

Melanie couldn't help but feel responsible. She fell to the floor and hung up the phone. Sobbing she prayed that he hadn't hit the tree on purpose. *It was just an accident. It wasn't because of her email. Maybe he hadn't even read it yet.*

The next morning, she realized that her prayers were unheard. Sure enough, she had an email from Ryan sent at 12:30 am less than 30 minutes after she sent her message.

"I can't believe you won't forgive me. I love you; don't you get that? I made a horrible mistake and I hurt you. I will never ever hurt you again. I don't want to be alive without you. I don't want to be with anyone else. You're my life. You make my whole life and I have no life without you in it. I hope that you're happy with your decision, but just know that I've never been so sorry. I can't even imagine my life without you in it and I don't ever want to."

After Ryan died, Melanie just kind of fell apart. She couldn't stop blaming herself. She tried to see a counselor, but it didn't really help. Her mom tried to help, but she just didn't understand how Melanie felt responsible.

"Mel, I know you're sad, but honey you didn't do this. He was spiraling out of control before you broke up with him."

Still, Melanie blamed herself.

Maybe if I had said something, told someone about the drugs and drinking, then maybe he would still be here.

She played the "what if" game in her mind, going over every detail 1000 times. Melanie didn't want to do anything. She didn't apply for advertising jobs like she should have been doing. She couldn't focus on anything except how she had "killed" Ryan.

Melanie daydreamed about their life in Durham, of how it was supposed to be. She felt cheated.

What if I had given him another chance? Would we be together now? Would we be happy?

As time went on, it seemed like she could only remember the good times in her relationship. She felt like sleep was the only place she was happy. That's how she spent most of her days. Laying in her bed, huddled up in his Abercrombie sweatshirt. Lifehouse's "You and Me" was on repeat. Her parents at work and Madison away at college, she could hide from reality in her room.

Her friends tried to help. They visited her, asked her to dinner and to go out.

One day, Sydney, frustrated with Melanie's desire to do anything but sleep said, "I am sorry about Ryan. I can't imagine what it feels like to lose someone you loved, but you are still alive and you need to start acting like it. Ryan made you happy sometimes, but a lot of the time, he could be a real jerk. When you were with him, it was like you weren't you. You didn't have an opinion or a say in anything. I am sorry he died, but I thought if you broke up for good, then maybe I would get my friend back."

Melanie sat there staring at her, speechless.

She's right. I was the one to break up with him. I was the one who was angry at him for ruining everything we had together. I just let his death make me forget everything.

Melanie's parents continued to support her, but they were worried.

"Honey, you're going to have to make a new plan. You can't just live here forever, not working, not going to school. We can help you decide what you want to do, but you have to do something."

Melanie agreed and started applying for jobs. Slowly, she began to live her life again. She reconnected with old friends. She started working out at the local gym, trying a variety of workout classes. She started going out with friends again. She started talking about the future. She started making plans. She just started living again.

Chapter 4

2014

Clayton grabbed Melanie's hand as she walked him to the door saying, "Good night, pretty girl. I'll see you in the morning."

"Hey, I told you. Do not worry about me. I can easily take an Uber to the airport."

"It's fine. I moved my appointments. I promise I'm free and besides you know you can barely carry your suitcase by yourself."

Not able to argue with that last comment, she agreed as he grabbed her with both arms. Enveloping her in a big hug, he kissed her softly on the lips and then again on the forehead. She kissed him back and thanked him, thinking how thoughtful he was.

Thankful he did not overstay his welcome when she had packing to do, she decided to get busy. Opening her bedroom door, she heard meowing. She realized her cat, Desi, had wandered into her closet and gotten stuck there. She rescued the ball of fur, petting her head and stroking her ears.

"Oh, I am so sorry, sweet girl. I didn't know you were in there."

Desi was meowing and purring, clearly accepting the apology as Melanie kept petting her. Desi was short for Desma and she was her best friend. She was the very first thing she bought when she moved to Florida. She knew she needed a companion in the apartment. When she first saw the yellow-haired ball of fur, she knew she was the one she had to have.

Relieved that her cat was safe and sound, she started opening drawers. The box still sitting on the floor caught her eye.

Underneath the postcards, something silver and sparkly caught her eye. She could almost make out the HAPPY BIRTHDAY letters when she realized it was from her 23rd birthday to Vegas. It was right after Ryan passed away. She didn't think she should be celebrating yet, but her friend Sarah had insisted. As she held the crown in her hand, she could almost feel the desert heat on her skin.

September 2009

As the black limousine pulled up to the curb, Sarah popped a surprise bottle of champagne. The Vegas skyline spread out in front of them. The girls toasted their glasses and found their way to their hotel room.

Melanie thought to herself, *I am glad I decided to go. This weekend is going to be amazing and Sarah was right. It is just what I needed to get away and have some fun.*

Sarah's dad had gotten them a free hotel suite and limo service. The girls' only job was to drink and have fun. Melanie was grateful for Sarah's friendship. She didn't feel like celebrating even if it was her birthday weekend, but how could she say no to a free trip?

"I'm so glad we stayed friends even after I transferred. I was kind of worried we wouldn't stay in touch when I moved."

"Me too. We will always be friends. Besides, I knew you wouldn't stay gone for long."

"What? What do you mean?"

"Ryan wasn't the guy for you. I knew that. I just couldn't tell you that. You weren't yourself when you were with him. The Melanie I know would never have moved for a guy."

"True. What was I ever thinking?"

"That if you moved everything would be better."

"Exactly, but it wasn't. It was actually awful a lot of the time. I just couldn't tell anyone. I still miss him all of the time though. What does that say about me?"

"That you loved him and you're a good person. Just know that I'm always here for you."

"Thank you for that and for this weekend."

"You're welcome. Now let's get ready. We've got dancing to do."

The girls curled their hair, trying on each other's dresses and singing to the radio. Melanie was happy for the vacation and the distraction from reality for a while.

Chapter 5

2014

Melanie, smiling at the memory of her special birthday weekend, remembered when her friendship with Sarah began.

It was at her college orientation day. Her parents had barely left the parking lot when the freshman class was expected to attend an assembly. Standing in a line that wrapped around the quad and back, Melanie was irritated. She wasn't so sure about going to this college. It was three hours from home. Most of her high school friends were going to a different one. She wondered if she would ever make friends.

Not really paying attention to her surroundings, she bumped into a girl in front of her. Not knowing what to say and desperately wanting to make friends, she complimented her purse.

It was a genuine compliment, but the girl's smile as she said "thank you" made her think *she seems really nice.*

After waiting in the long line together, the girls made plans to meet that evening. Melanie couldn't believe that one purse compliment had created a friendship that lasted almost ten years. Sarah was a part of so many of her memories.

October 2005

As Melanie removed her eyeliner and washed her face, Sarah entered the bathroom shared by all of the girls on her dorm floor. In the beginning, Melanie hated the lack of privacy, but it made for some interesting conversations before bed.

Sarah approached the sink asking, "So, how was the date?"

"Not the greatest. He literally only talked about himself. He wants to be a surgeon. He wouldn't even let me cut the bread."

"You're kidding? What do you mean, wouldn't let you?"

He grabbed the loaf of bread and the knife when the waitress brought it to the table. He looked at me and said, "I'll do it. I am going to be a surgeon."

"That is priceless. Oh God, I am sorry. That does sound awful. Was the dinner good at least?"

"Yes. Mine was delicious, but that's the other thing. He didn't even look at the menu."

"What? Why? Did he only eat bread?"

"No, he just asked for chicken fingers without even looking at the menu!"

"Wow! So, an arrogant bread surgeon who only eats off the kid's meal."

"Yep. Some date, huh?"

"Sorry, it went so badly. I am kind of happy though."

"Why are you happy?"

"Because Ben's friend Adam asked if you wanted to go on a double date sometime."

"Adam? Do I even know an Adam?"

"He was at the game with us last week."

"Oh, I remember him. Tall blonde guy, right?"

"Yep. That's the one."

"He's really cute, but I don't even think I said one word to him!"

"I guess he thought you were pretty. Either way it will be fun. What do you say?"

"As long as he's not planning on being a surgeon and as long as you go with me."

"Of course. That's the point of a double date."

She remembered Adam. Except for a few boys she went on dates with in high school, he was her first real boyfriend. Besides, having a boyfriend in college was so much more serious than one in high school. She could remember one of the first dates.

As Adam was walking her back to her dorm, it started to rain. She tried to use her hands as a make shift shield, darting through the pelting rain. As they ran, he grabbed her closer. Safe under the doorway awning, he reached down to kiss her. As the rain poured down around them, she kissed him back.

"I'll call you tomorrow after my test. We can go to a movie or something."

"I can't wait."

"I'll even let you pick the movie."

"Even better."

"Goodnight."

Still smiling at their goodbye, she was surprised to see Sarah standing in the dorm room entry way.

"So? How was your night?"

"Pshh, like you weren't just standing at the door, spying?"

"C'mon, you know I can barely see out of this window."

Sarah had a point, at 5' 2" she barely reached the peephole. Melanie at 5' 8" almost towered over her. Still, they had been practically inseparable since the first day of freshman orientation. Not knowing anyone at her college, Melanie was extremely grateful for such a quick and true friend. Happy with the prospect of another date, she filled Sarah in on the evening.

"I think I might really like him."

"I knew it. I could tell during our double date! Ben joked that we should just sneak away and see if you two noticed."

"Oh, come on, we weren't that obvious."

"Umm, you barely acknowledged that we were in the room."

"He's really nice and he doesn't just talk about himself."

"True and he's not a bread surgeon."

"Good point. Yes, he gets props for not being a bread surgeon."

She remembered how sad she had been when she realized they weren't as serious as she had hoped. How she had cried and Sarah had given her some great advice.

Melanie pointed at the computer screen. Showing Sarah, the messages.

"Look, you can read it all right there."

"Wait, so this random girl just started messaging you?"

"Yep. She said her name is Ali and that she is Adam's neighbor. See, you can read it all for yourself. I guess they've been a thing for months."

"No way. He really likes you. I know that and so does Ben."

"Well, he must really like her too."

"No way. She is totally making this up."

"She sounds pretty serious."

"Oh gosh, she's sending pictures of them now."

"I knew it was too good to be true."

"Don't say that. You deserve a good guy. I'm just sorry that he's not."

"No kidding. I totally got played."

"Are you sure you're okay?"

"Yep. Just fine."

Melanie was trying hard not to let her disappointment show, but Sarah could tell her friend was hurt. She hugged her saying, "No boy is worth your tears and the one who is won't make you cry."

Melanie hugged her back, thankful for her advice and her support.

"Thanks."

"Besides, the best thing about college is there are lots of guys. You'll find another one and this one will be worth your time. Promise."

Chapter 6
2014

She rummaged through the box, the piles of pictures and memories. So many pictures; so many memories.

A picture of her high school friends, all smiling, standing on a rickety porch. She knew that was the night she met Ryan. She could almost smell the stale beer and hear the shouting over the loud music.

How they met was so random. She wasn't even supposed to be at that party.

She made a last-minute decision to go to a college party with her friends from home. She had plans to go somewhere else that weekend, but her girlfriends were too convincing. Worried she was losing touch with her high school friends, she made the three-hour trip home.

She didn't even know the guys hosting the party. Her friends did though. They introduced them as Ryan and Mike. Their house was full of people. It seemed to be the college party house. There were kegs in the living room and even a beach with real sand in the basement.

Her high school friends seemed to know everyone in the house. They quickly paired up with the boys they liked, leaving Melanie alone and regretting her decision to come along.

Getting bored, she joined in on a game of beer pong. The only person she knew playing was Ryan. She didn't really know him. She had only seen him around their hometown a few times. Even so, she joined the game and agreed to be his partner.

They ended up being a pretty great team. With every score, they toasted their solo cups. As the game wound down, they went outside where they started talking. She told him about college and how she was just visiting for the weekend. He told her about his dream of being a doctor. She didn't take him seriously at first.

She didn't know he had more goals than just having a kegerator in the kitchen.

As it grew closer to daylight and her friends got cozy with their dates, she found herself wanting to get to know him even more.

Slow dancing to Lifehouse, he leaned in to kiss her. She kissed him back and knew this was the beginning of something special.

She was so excited after meeting him, he seemed to really care about her. After Adam two-timed her, she thought a nice boy from her hometown would be much better than any of the city boys at her own college.

Thanksgiving break was only a few weeks after that first party. Ryan started texting her and they kept in touch the whole time. Melanie remembered how nervous she was as she curled her hair. She could remember listening to Colbie Caillat's "Bubbly" as she put on her makeup.

That's how I feel, she thought. Her stomach was full of butterflies. Ryan was home visiting for the holiday break and he had asked her on a date.

She spent almost an hour trying to decide on an outfit. Picking her denim Hollister skirt and gray Abercrombie tank top, she asked her sister Madison for another opinion.

"Your skirt is really short, but I like your hair. Where are you going?"

"On a date."

"Oh, with who?"

"Ryan. You'll meet him soon."

Texting every day, she got to know him better. He was actually pretty funny and she could find herself really starting to like him. Their texting turned into nightly phone calls. It had been almost a month since she had seen him in person and she was nervous.

As she put in her earrings and sprayed her wrists with her new Paris Hilton perfume, she heard the doorbell downstairs.

She remembered how it started out great. He was funny and sweet and really seemed to like her. She could be herself around him, but then things started to change.

He started to accuse her of cheating. When she was being nothing but faithful. She would call him every night before going to sleep. No matter the time or that her time zone was an hour ahead.

He needed constant reassurance. She should have seen that as a warning flag, but he blamed the distance. She could remember their first Christmas as an official couple.

49

They should have been so happy. She was transferring to be closer to him. Melanie tried to hold the tape with one finger while grabbing the slick paper with another finger. It didn't work. She cut the paper too short. Frustrated, she yelled for her younger sister Madison's help.

Madison held the tape while Melanie secured the paper.

"What time do you have to leave?"

"I need to be at Ryan's grandpa's by 4:00, but I work until three, so I need to hurry and get these presents wrapped."

It was her first Christmas with her boyfriend Ryan and she wanted to make a good impression on his family.

Her younger sister Madison shook her head.

"I know I'm younger and all, but are you sure you want to go to Christmas with Ryan's family? For one, Christmas isn't for another five days. Why do they have to have their Christmas so early anyway? Don't you think you'll see him enough now that you're going to his school?"

"Madison, he has a big family. They have lots of different Christmas's. Someday you will understand. You're supposed to go to your boyfriend's family Christmas even if it is five days before the actual day. If I didn't go to all of them then it would just look bad."

"Whatever you say, but mom and dad are seriously not happy you're switching schools. I heard mom tell dad 'you're changing yourself for a guy.'"

"What? Mom said that?"

"Yeah, I heard them talking in the kitchen the other night. Mom said she's worried about you."

"Why is she worried about me? I am twenty-one years old. I have been living in a different state three hours from home. She should be happy I am moving closer and that I'm happy."

"Well, you guys don't sound happy. I heard you on the phone last night. You sounded mad."

The comment angered Melanie. How could her mom think that? Ryan didn't make her do anything. She was choosing to move. She wasn't changing herself. Her friends from high school go to that school too. The only person she had at her college was Sarah and she was way too busy with Ben to spend time with her anymore.

Switching schools wasn't an easy decision, but she knew that moving and being closer to Ryan would be the best thing for their relationship. They had been fighting because of the distance. Once she was in the same town, things would be so much better.

Only, things didn't get better. Melanie wished she would have taken her sister's comments more seriously. She never should have transferred. Her mom tried to tell her; her friends tried to stop her.

She remembered the first time her friends told her they didn't like Ryan.

July 2007

Melanie said goodbye to her friends. She never should have gone to this party with them in the first place. Her phone rang in her purse.

"Seriously, why is he calling again?" her friend Macie whined.

"He's just worried about me and wants me to stay with him."

"Um, no, he's worried you're going to realize how much better you are than him and dump his ass." Bridget chimed in.

Melanie couldn't believe her friends right now. These were the same friends who introduced her to Ryan and convinced her to go with them to the party at his house.

"I thought you liked Ryan."

"Uh, yeah to party with, not for our friend to date." Macie said.

"He is seriously super controlling. Like you're not you when he's around."

"He's not even with us and he's taking over the whole night. You're leaving before 11. They haven't even set off the good fireworks yet."

Melanie thought to herself, *They are just drunk and jealous. I have someone who loves me who wants to be with me. I don't need to hit on random guys at random parties anymore.*

As she walked to her car, she heard a familiar voice. Drake was home!

"Mel! Is that you? Are you home for the summer?"

"Nope, just the weekend."

"Me too. Taking a red eye to Hawaii tomorrow night. Mom wants a family vacation before we all grow up and move away."

"Hawaii sounds amazing. I'm going to the Ozarks with Ryan's family tomorrow morning."

Melanie lost track of time caught up in the familiar conversation.

"How's the new school? Do you like it?"

Melanie wanted to tell him the truth. She wanted to tell everyone. She knew she made a mistake. She never should have moved. The fighting with Ryan hadn't gotten better. It had only gotten worse. She couldn't say that though.

"School is good. I am going to graduate earlier than planned. I have an internship all summer. It's pretty cool. I am making this whole marketing campaign for a winery down there. I just took off the week to go with Ryan's family. I'll be back again for Labor Day. What about you? How's school? What's the plan after graduation?"

"No plan yet. Pops wants me to take over the company. Not sure I am ready to settle down and move home just yet. Visiting is one thing, but living here is another story."

"I know what you mean. That's a big decision to make working for the company and moving home. If you're back here for Labor Day, let me know. It's my birthday."

"Mel, I know when your birthday is, but I won't be home."

"Oh, okay just if you change your mind, a bunch of my friends from school are coming to visit. It should be fun."

"I'm sure it will be, but I have to go to San Fran to some big conference with my pops. You still haven't visited me yet. Why don't you plan a visit?"

Melanie laughed and promised to visit as her phone rang for the third time. She knew it was Ryan and she knew she needed to leave. He was drinking again and needed a ride. She knew he would need to get some sleep. Otherwise, she knew they wouldn't leave for the Ozarks before noon. She also knew that she would not be visiting Drake at school. Ryan didn't understand their friendship. He thought there was more to it than just being friends.

I shouldn't visit him anyway. He has a girlfriend and I have Ryan. Even if things have been kind of bad lately, things will be better on vacation. When we aren't at school and so busy with internship and studying.

She hugged Drake goodbye and left the party to meet Ryan.

Chapter 7

2014

Looking back at that night, she realized she chose Ryan over everyone. "I put him first in front of my family, my friends, everything I believed in. I put my own dreams on hold and only focused on us. I tried to fix a relationship that wasn't supposed to ever be fixed."

She remembered that Ozarks trip. He drank so much; they fought the entire time. She didn't understand why she couldn't see how bad his drinking had gotten until it was too late.

Why was I so blind to see all of the problems?

The more she remembered the more determined she was to never find herself in a situation like that again. It was remembering the bad things that helped her overcome her guilt.

"It was part of the process," her therapist had said. As tears streamed down her cheeks, she remembered another Christmas break.

Jan 2007

Melanie sat sipping her beer while Ryan joked around with his friends. She was annoyed. It was her Christmas break and she had friends she wanted to see. He promised they would meet with her friends after they met his friends for one drink. That was four hours ago.

"Come on. Seriously, I always do what you want. Will you just come with me?"

"Babe, I said I would soon."

"Ryan, it's been four hours. My friends are all going to be leaving."

Melanie angrily sat on a barstool wishing she had driven separately. *Why didn't I just take my car? I knew this would happen. Every time Ryan drinks with his friends nothing else matters.*

Worried that she wouldn't see her friends even when she was home, she tried texting her friends to meet her instead. But everyone was waiting for her at a different bar. She called for a taxi, but the wait was too long. Melanie put the phone back in her purse just as her beer bottle went flying. It slid across the bar before shattering in a mess on the floor.

Ryan was drunk once again and making a scene. The bartender tried to talk to him calmly, but he started yelling.

Melanie paid for their drinks and pulled him to the car. Her friends were forgotten and once again she was Ryan's babysitter.

Chapter 8
2014

"Okay, time to get a grip," Melanie said to no one but Desi. Her furry companion sprawled out on top of her still empty suitcase.

"That's right Desi. I need to pack. Thanks for reminding me," she said to the cat, happy that she had chosen the top suitcase for her bed.

"No more distractions."

She turned on the radio and started folding clothes. She made some progress on her suitcase. Only a few small things to add in the morning.

I can finish the rest tomorrow, she thought.

Lying in bed, her nerves started to get the best of her. She realized she had barely seen Drake Jameson since their "hookup" almost four years ago. What seemed like a good idea at the time had really just made a mess of their friendship. She didn't know what to do.

Her mind wandered and she was suddenly thinking about that night.

Melanie followed Drake up the Jameson's long driveway. When she opened her car door, he was waiting with his hand outstretched.

"Shhh! Let's just go to the pool house. If my parents see you, we will never get away."

She laughed as he held her hand and led her through the dark backyard into the pool house.

She kept thinking to herself, *I seriously wish I would have brought a swimsuit.*

She felt nervous and second guessed her decision coming here as Drake walked out with a bottle of champagne. Her nerves started to calm as he poured her a glass.

"Pretty sure this is supposed to be saved for a special occasion, but what the hell. Here's to old friends!"

They clinked glasses as he turned down the lights and opened the hot tub cover.

Wearing only her underwear and bra she quickly got in the warm water. At first, she felt awkward. Trying to calm her nerves, she kept drinking. They talked about life. What his plan was now that he graduated.

"Well, I am actually leaving for Japan this week. I was going to tell you that earlier, but it just never came up."

"When do you come back?"

"Not sure yet. It kind of depends on how business is over there. I think it will probably be a month."

As the champagne bubbles went to her head, Drake kissed her. As she kissed him back, he unhooked her bra. She wrapped her legs around him as he pushed her against the side of the hot tub. Lost in the moment, neither one tried to stop what was happening.

She couldn't tell if it was the champagne or if she had feelings for Drake after all of this time. Either way, she didn't mean to take it that far. Regret filling her mind, he erased her doubts as he said, "You can stay if you want?"

They lay talking as she fell asleep next to him, feeling safe and happy with her best friend by her side.

Chapter 9

She thought getting with Drake would be an easy rebound, but she realized that she really did like him. At first, she felt like she was betraying Ryan, but then she wondered if maybe she should have been with Drake all along. What if she had made some crazy mistake and missed her fate with Drake? She wouldn't have been through the heartache and her life would have been like the fairytale she always wanted.

She texted him later that afternoon asking, "Do you want to do something tonight?" She hoped when he returned from Japan, they could pick up where they left off. She was happy and excited about the idea of a relationship for the first time since Ryan died.

Except Drake never let her know. He left for Japan without saying goodbye. She didn't know what to do.

She remembered how enlivened she felt telling Sydney about Drake.

"So, I have news." Melanie told her.

"Wait. You haven't taken the LSAT yet? Right? I have it down on my calendar in two weeks."

"No, you're right about that, although not sure why you have it on YOUR calendar, but yes in two weeks. Please don't remind me."

"I just want to make sure I'm there to give you moral support. Okay. So then, what's your news?"

"I think I really like someone."

"What? Who? Someone new?"

"Not new. Drake."

"Drake? Jameson? That's not new. This is your big epiphany, that you like Drake. Are you kidding me? You always liked him even when you were with Ryan. You two have been crazy about each other for years. Everyone knows that. Well, I guess everyone but you."

"Sure, it is. We've just been friends before."

She blushed as she remembered the time in the hot tub. How being with Drake didn't feel awkward. She didn't have to be someone else. She could just be herself.

"Well, from the smile on your face, I'd say you're more than friends now?"

"I don't know. He left for Japan and I haven't talked to him."

"Well, what are you waiting for? Call him."

Feeling confident and happy with her friend's reaction to her news, she wanted to talk to Drake. She tried calling, but no answer.

Must be the time difference, she thought to herself.
She had thought that things were really going to work out. They could pick up right where they left off ten years ago.

After texting and calling him a few times, she was feeling disappointed. If he did respond, it was only short

61

answers. Or no answer at all. She tried to stay busy studying for the LSAT and working out at the gym.

Grateful for the distraction, she was thankful for her job and her upcoming test.

She laughed thinking, *Back when I thought studying for the LSAT was hard.*

She could remember telling her parents her dream of going to law school.

It's a new year. It's time to make some new goals. It's time to stop being sad and start creating my own life.

Melanie researched law schools, read what the LSAT entailed and realized she was ready for a new plan.

"Mom, Dad, I know what I want to do."

"That's great honey. Did you find an advertising job you want?"

"Nope. I want to go to law school."

"Really? Are you sure?"

"Yeah, I wanted to a while ago, but Ryan's dreams kind of took over. I've been looking up schools and I ordered an LSAT book to start studying."

"I think this is great. You definitely need a new dream."

Chapter 10

Happy with her decision and grateful for her parent's support, Melanie was excited about the future for the first time in a long time. She had the LSAT to prepare for and hopefully a new relationship with her oldest and best friend, Drake. She held onto that hope until she ran into him at the gym.

Fresh from a cardio class, Melanie was hardly paying attention. She bent down to tie her shoes and saw familiar green eyes. She could barely form a sentence.

Drake was home. He was here. He was in America. He was in her hometown. In her gym. Standing right in front of her. She awkwardly tried to hug him and he reciprocated an equally awkward gesture.

"Um, hi. When did you get home?"

"Oh, a few days ago. Sorry. I meant to call you."

"Oh, that's nice. Yeah, I've been pretty busy taking my test and working."

She didn't even hear him say goodbye. She hoped he couldn't see how upset she was. Inside she was fuming. She barely made it into the parking lot before the tears started falling. She called Sydney, crying. Her friend barely got a word in before Melanie started explaining.

"He didn't even tell me he was home from Japan. I'm just so mad."

Sydney tried to help, "Maybe you should just talk to him? Maybe there's more to the story?"

"No, I never want to talk to Drake Jameson again. How can he be so important to me and then act like I don't even exist? I don't matter at all."

Her friend tried to help, but Melanie just wanted to be alone.

She thought to herself, *I put myself out there. I am not the kind of girl who asks the guys out first.* Remembering how Drake had hurt her made her appreciate Clayton even more.

Trying to sleep, she started to imagine the wedding this weekend. She knew Kate had impeccable taste. After all, she was an assistant buyer at Barney's New York in Chicago; and to the Jamesons, money was no object. Especially to Daniel and Drake's mother Veronica. She lived to decorate and loved any opportunity to have a party. This wedding was going to be the wedding of the year. Her family had two rooms at The Waldorf and she knew the hotel was booked with guests for the Newman-Jameson wedding.

She fell asleep dreaming of Kate's one of a kind Vivienne Westwood gown.

Chapter 11

Soon her alarm clock was beeping. Awake, she remembered her flight and ran to the shower. She quickly blow-dried her hair and got dressed.

Rolling her suitcase into the living room, she saw Desi chewing on something in the corner. Grabbing the bent and now partially eaten photograph, she remembered the night the picture was taken.

It was the last night she saw Drake Jameson. She had her favorite black dress on and it was cold. She remembered being very cold. She wore her red peacoat. She was worried she would lose it that night, but surprisingly she managed to keep a hold of it.

Thinking about that night, she could almost taste the salt on her lips and the tequila burning her throat.

After the gym run in, Melanie avoided Drake. She didn't want any chance of running into him. Then one weekend everything changed.

While visiting her friends in the city for the weekend, she unexpectedly ran into Drake and a few of their mutual friends. Everything was fine in the beginning and Melanie paid more attention to his friends than to him. She sat as far away as possible.

She tried to ignore him but Drake wouldn't have that.

What is he doing? Melanie thought as he bought her a shot. She didn't even have time to respond.

She thought, *What the hell?* as she took the shot.

He can waste his money on me. Before she walked away, he put his arm around her. He handed Melanie: a salt shaker, a lime, and a shot of Patron. Instead of sucking the lime at the end of the shot he kissed Melanie. Melanie was so confused, but she didn't push him away. Instead, she kissed him back.

The tequila trance was broken as she looked at her irritated friends. Aware of how he hurt her feelings not that long ago, they practically scolded her. "We did not come to the city to hang out with Drake Jameson and his friends. We could do that at home. We wasted a perfectly great night when we could have been meeting new guys."

They basically dragged her out of the bar and into the cab. She didn't blame them though. She couldn't believe she was kissing Drake Jameson again after he had ignored her for so long. It's like she would never learn.

Still when she thought about that night, shivers went down her spine. It was just so unexpected when she walked into that unknown bar and saw him sitting there. She spent most of the night trying not to even glance in his direction. It wasn't just the unexpected kiss after the tequila shot. He kept kissing her even as her friends got into the cab.

It was snowing and she remembered looking up at the sky and thinking, *This is how love is supposed to be.* Maybe it was the tequila, or maybe it was fate. Either way it felt like magic. No matter how hard she tried to push Drake Jameson out of her mind, he kept coming back.

Chapter 12

2014

The picture back in the box where it belonged, she gave Desi a treat as she thought to herself, *Why do I even have that box? I have a whole box of memories I just need to let go of.*

Her thoughts were interrupted with a knock at the door. She heard Clayton's familiar voice, "Hi ya, pretty girl. You ready to go?"

Before she could respond, he grabbed her suitcase and had it safely stowed in the back of his black Navigator. She barely got her key in the lock before he was starting the ignition.

The drive to the airport wasn't long and there wasn't much traffic. Despite her feelings surrounding Drake, she was excited for the weekend. Following the sign to departures, he grabbed her hand.

"I'm just sorry I can't go this weekend. Make sure you send me a picture in this dress I've heard so much about."

She laughed, "I just hope it still fits."

"I'm sure you will look beautiful. Have fun with your family and I'll see you when you get back."

She checked her luggage and went in search of a Starbucks. The line was practically out the door, but she really needed a quick pick-me-up. Luckily, the line moved rather quickly and she sipped her warm, caramel Macchiato, in search of a seat. It was going to be a long day. The only flight she could find that allowed her to make it to the city before dinner had two layovers. She planned to make the most of her time. She had her study materials, a few trashy magazines and her favorite Emily Giffin book, *Love the One You're With* in her carry-on. She knew she should use this time to study, but she loved to read in her free time. Even though she had read all of Emily Giffin's books five times over, she still looked forward to reading if Ellen chose to stay with her husband Andy or run away with her ex-boyfriend Leo.

Melanie loved books and she enjoyed everything from James Patterson's murder mysteries to Cecily von Ziegesar's Gossip Girl series, but her favorites were Emily Giffin and Jane Green books. These books gave her hope for real romance. What happened with Ryan was an awful tragedy, but it didn't mean she was to be alone her whole life. It had been almost six years. It was time that she really moved on and let her beaten heart heal.

Chapter 13

Drake

Drake Jameson checked his watch for the seventh time in 30 minutes. He needed to leave work in 15 minutes to make the four-hour-drive to the city. His older brother, Daniel, was getting married this weekend and his bachelor party was tonight. His bags were packed and waiting in his black Escalade, parked out front of his office. He sent some last-minute emails and headed for the parking lot.

He was pretty nervous about the weekend. Daniel's fiancée, Kate, was great. That was not the problem. He was worried about seeing Melanie Dickson this weekend. Melanie had always been "his" girl. They had been friends for as long as he could remember. Growing up she was his best friend and they were practically inseparable. As they got older, they stayed friends, but weren't as close. Melanie started dating "bad" boys from the next town over and their wild partying didn't really mix well with his private school entourage. Sometimes they would run into each other and every time he saw her, it was like no time had passed.

She always gave him the biggest hug and made him feel like he was the most special guy in the world. Then came the hookup four years ago. He had pretty much ignored her after that and now he felt like a complete jerk. It didn't help that he literally left for Japan not even two days after they slept together. He didn't know what to do. Should he send flowers and say thanks for a great sendoff? I'll see you in six months? No, that made it sound like a business transaction. Or that he wasn't into her? Or that it wasn't special?

He really liked Melanie. He just didn't know how to say it. He thought about that night she stayed over. He knew their decision complicated the friendship. He knew he should have stopped it. He could tell she had feelings that night. He never should have asked her to stay. He wasn't ready for a relationship, especially with her. Not then at least. He didn't know what he wanted. He was living two different lives. In Japan, he could be anyone he wanted. No one knew him. He remembered how Melanie called him a few times when he was in Japan.

He didn't know what to say to her. He didn't know what he wanted. He was trying to focus on work and building his business. He didn't have the time for a relationship.

Drake
2010

Drake Jameson slammed another Saki bomb. His first few days in Japan were pretty uneventful. His job was important to him and he wanted the employees to take him seriously. When he joined the family technology business, he had to earn people's respect. They just saw some spoiled, punk-ass kid whose daddy handed him a big boy job. He didn't want any special treatment. He made a point to work in the factory, breaking down boxes, sorting parts, just doing anything that needed to be done. During the week he worked hard.

But weekends were a different story. At his factory, most workers didn't work Monday or Friday. Which meant an extra-long weekend. Japanese bars didn't close until after 5 am. Something he needed to get used to, but was quickly learning. As he threw another wad of cash on the table, his phone vibrated in his pocket. Glancing at the caller id he saw that it was Melanie. He knew he should answer, but what would he say.

How did he get himself in such a mess? He didn't know how to tell Melanie he wasn't ready to settle down. His ex-girlfriend Tiffani was calling him at all hours of the day, too, asking if they could talk, if they could work things out.

He downed another shot and let the call go to voicemail. Melanie was his "someday" girl, but he just wasn't ready to settle down. He had been on again off again with his girlfriend from college, Tiffani. He knew she wasn't good for him, but still he never broke up with her for long, even when he had practically caught her cheating on him multiple times. He didn't know what it was about her, but she sure was fun. She definitely wasn't marriage material, but hey, when you're 23, who is thinking about marriage? It's all about a good time, right?

Chapter 14

Melanie

When the plane was only 15 minutes from landing, she was already daydreaming about the weekend.

She found her carousel just in time to watch her luggage go around once more. She grabbed it as her cell phone rang. She instantly knew it was Kate and followed the sign to O'Hare Arrival Pick Up. Sure enough, a long, white limo was waiting and Kate, along with three other girls, leaped out to greet her.

The driver helped her with her bags and Kate poured her a glass of champagne. She had a feeling this weekend was going to be really fun. The limo took them to their last dress fitting before the ceremony. Melanie loved her dress when they had ordered it last winter and was happy. She still felt the same seven months later. The floor length, black satin, A-line gown cascaded down her sun-kissed body, making her skin glow and her fresh highlights look glossy. She twirled in the mirror and Kate squealed with delight.

After all the girls had tried on their dresses, they checked into their hotel rooms to get ready for dinner at one of Melanie's favorite restaurants, MK Chicago. After going through her suitcase twice, she finally decided on a form-fitting jersey wrap dress and gold leather wedges. She added some gold hoops, gave some more definition to her eyes, and teased her hair. There was giggling outside of her door and then she heard, "Are you decent?"

She grabbed her clutch and met three similarly dressed girls in the hallway. Kate had on a sequined skirt instead of a dress. She had always loved "fun" skirts and tonight was no exception. Their dinner was amazing and as she sipped her pinot noir, she thought about how happy she was with her life at this point.

It was such a change from the way she used to feel. The first two years after graduation and Ryan's death, she felt absolutely, completely worthless. Going back to school was definitely a wise decision. They ordered another bottle of wine as the other girls told embarrassing stories about Daniel and Kate during their college years. All of the girls had been her roommate and one of them was still, well at least until after the wedding. Then she was to look for a new one because Kate was moving into Daniel's condo in the city.

Melanie couldn't help but be a tiny bit jealous. After all, Kate had a Jameson boy and with that came the lifestyle. After finishing four bottles of wine, the girls headed to their first stop, MAX, for martinis. Melanie was already feeling pretty good and was trying to remember the last time she had drank so heavily.

Since moving to Florida and not knowing anyone, in addition to practically drowning in casework, it had been a few years since she had been able to relax and really enjoy herself. She was happy she was able to spend this special night with her friend and couldn't help but wonder if the whole weekend was going to be like this. After practically gulping three martinis, Kate announced that they were going to McFadden's. Melanie opted for a beer and surprisingly, vodka-loving Kate did too.

Chapter 15

Drake

Driving to the city, Drake had a lot of time to think. He knew he messed up. He should have called Melanie to explain, but living in Japan, what was the point? He was gone more than he was home. It was his work ethic that kept him juggling life overseas. His dad was getting too old to travel for such a long period of time. The Japanese tech market was too important not to have someone there full time.

Drake stepped up when his family needed him. It was his work in Japan that kept the family business growing. Living such a double life, it was easy to put off settling down. The girls over there were wild and they loved him. He could practically walk in a bar and have any girl he wanted. His blond hair was like a magnet for the Japanese girls and it didn't hurt that he pretty much lived in one of the nicest hotels over there.

In Japan he could be anyone he wanted and no one knew about his family or his job or anything. He was a mystery and those Japanese girls? They loved a mystery. After a while, the party life got old, especially when he came home. Most of his high school friends were working and living in their hometown, married to their high school girlfriends and settling down.

He had to admit it, sometimes that life looked pretty good, especially on Sunday nights, when his friends considered it a family day. That is when he would start to get lonely. Sure, he could call Tiffani and have her down for the weekend, but deep down he knew Tiffani's biggest attraction to him was not him, but his family, more so the business and the lifestyle that came with it.

Every time she came to visit, she would start acting completely fake and talked down to everyone, even the waitress at Steak N' Shake. He could not stand rudeness, just because you may have money does not mean you can order people around like they are your servants. The more time Tiffani would spend in his hometown, the less he could see himself with her and he wondered why he was even with her; this was a major turnoff. Still, he kept her around.

His thoughts were interrupted by his phone buzzing in the cup holder. It was Daniel asking all about the details of the night.

He just said, "Relax, I am on my way and I have this handled. I'll see you in a while. Be ready to party."

His work in Japan was finished. He was able to hire someone else to take over after he got the factory up and going.

Coming home for good, he was ready to start settling down. He wanted to tell Melanie how he really felt, but she had moved away. He knew he was mostly to blame, and he should've told her how he really felt years ago. He had more than enough chances, but still something stopped him.

He remembered when he unexpectedly saw her in the city. He was just hanging out at a dive bar with his friends. He looked up and there she was, laughing, playing darts with his friends. She had always been pretty, but he remembered that night she had this red coat on and a little black dress. Her legs looked like they never stopped. She was hot. He always thought that, but more than her looks, she was special. He couldn't act like he didn't care anymore. He walked right up to her, put his arm around her shoulder, and bought two shots of tequila. The shots started to blur and he found himself almost saying, "I love you."

He could still remember the surprised look on her face when he kissed her. He was practically stammering, "I love you," so he grabbed the tequila shot instead.

He threw his lime down and instead of sucking the lime at the end of the shot he kissed her. Not just a friendly, hey there kind of kiss either. He full on grabbed her face and kissed her with all he had.

When he looked at her, she was so surprised, but it was a good kind of surprise. He forgot how happy she made him and how much he liked to make her smile. He didn't say how he felt, he thought the kiss did a better job than words. Only her friends were not pleased with their make out session. He could tell, they practically pulled her out of the bar and into the cab. He should have said it then.

He remembered he kissed her as they were standing against the cab and her friends were telling her she needed to go with them. The cab driver definitely wasn't helping. Drake still remembered what he said, "Listen, girl, you either go with him, or you go with them, but I'm not sitting here while you decide what you want."

Melanie kissed Drake back and left with her friends. He just stood there standing in the street with the snow falling. He was confused at how he let her get away again. One minute he was standing there looking into her brown eyes. He remembered she had snow in her hair and little snowflakes on her eyelashes and it was like she was this twinkly, sparkly dream. Then just as suddenly as she had been back in his arms, she disappeared. She chose her friends and left him all alone again.

Why was I so stupid and why couldn't I just man up and say how I felt? Seriously, it's Mel. What was the worst that could happen? She knows me better than most of my friends.

Why couldn't she just know how he felt, without him having to explain it? That was the issue. He didn't know how to explain it. It's like this kind of crazy love you never expect to continue twenty years later. Still, here he was thinking about Melanie Dickson and how he missed his shot. Now it was too late, because according to Facebook, Melanie was practically living with some douchebag doctor. He couldn't help but feel a little jealous; she was his girl, so what if he never told her, she should know this.

He didn't have much time to think. He could see the Waldorf as he drove into the city. He quickly checked into his room, and got ready for the night out.

He couldn't help but feel nervous about seeing Melanie. After all it had been four years. He secretly wondered if the familiar, old feelings would come rushing back or not. He told himself that it didn't matter how he felt. He had been the dumbass who let her get away.

If Mel was happy now, that was all that mattered. So, what if she had been his best friend and that he had known they would be together since kindergarten? Melanie Dickson was amazing. She was beautiful, smart, and she could be put in any situation and always have a good time. He knew she was perfect wife material, but Melanie did have one flaw. She had horrible taste in men, if they could even be called that.

Her ex-boyfriend Ryan was a complete asshole. He couldn't believe he died. He felt bad, but he was not nice to Melanie. He knew that. Hell, practically the whole town knew that. Melanie had good friends, but some of them had big mouths. When he heard that Ryan had hit her, he was happy he was dead, because he wanted to kill him. She deserved to finally be happy and if this douchebag doctor made her happy, well then, good for her. He knew he had missed his chance. So, the next best thing was to be happy for his friend. Melanie was his friend. She always had been and if that's all she ever would be, then that was better than nothing.

He remembered how one time he was in a huge fight with his parents about college, in particular, how he didn't want to go. On top of that he had recently wrecked his car.

It was an accident, but it was just another reason for them to say he was irresponsible and not mature enough to make big decisions. He was grounded for weeks, and his friends stopped calling. He wasn't supposed to have friends over, but Mel came by. They just hung out. They made popcorn, watched movies in the theater room, and ate cookie dough. She just listened to him and made him laugh. He couldn't remember if she had a boyfriend at the time or not. He was pretty sure he did have a girlfriend, but it didn't matter. Nothing happened though, because they were just friends and boy did he ever need one then.

There was a knock at the door and Daniel walked in along with his friend Ben, Kate's brother Connor, and two more of his high school friends. Daniel was already drinking Tanqueray and Ben poured some scotch. The guys toasted to Daniel and Kate and to a great weekend. Then they headed to grab something to eat and hit the bars.

Chapter 16

Melanie

Melanie remembered one of the first times Kate had visited Daniel in their hometown and she had chosen Melanie's Bud Light over Daniel's Coors Light and the ongoing argument over which brand was the best. She realized that was almost five years ago and she tried to figure out where the time had gone. Her thoughts were interrupted by one of the other bridesmaids, Holli, yelling, "It's dance time!" The girls danced to about ten songs, everything from "Sweet Caroline" to "Benny and the Jets" and even "Baby Got Back."

Melanie was laughing and trying not to be pulled to the ground by Holli when she looked up to familiar faces. Daniel's bachelor party had surprisingly ended up at the same bar as the girls.

One of the girls was mad saying, "Kate, this is a girls' only night! No boyfriends, husbands, or fiancées allowed!"

But when one of the groomsmen, Ben, put his arm around her and bought her a drink, she quickly forgot about the no-boys rule.

Melanie gave Drake a hug and looked up into all too familiar green eyes. She didn't know what to say. She wanted to tell him how sorry she was that she had been such a bad friend, that she should've called. She wanted to tell him that she wished they never had hooked up.

She wanted to tell him that she was sorry for making such a mess of their friendship, but all she could say was, "Hi."

He gave her a hug and said, "Hi, Mel. Wow! Florida has been good to you! You look awesome!"

Their reunion was interrupted by a tray of Jager bombs and Drake handed her one, clinking her glass and saying, "To old, but great friends."

She gulped her shot down and the dance party continued. Her cell phone buzzed and it was Clayton just calling to check in. She told him how much fun she was having, that she would call him tomorrow before the rehearsal, and that she missed him, too. She hung up feeling happy and thinking that with any other guy she might try to hide her inebriation a little, but Clayton liked her to relax and have a good time.

She was thinking about how nice of a guy she had and how he really did care about her even if she didn't want to admit it. As the bar emptied out, Kate and Daniel were in a corner kissing and talking. Holli was sitting on Ben's lap, giggling, and the other two girls were on their cell phones.

Melanie really wanted to ask Kate if the limo could come pick them up, but she didn't want to disturb the happy couple. So, she decided to go to the restroom instead, worried about how she looked after drinking for over eight hours. Surprised that she still looked pretty decent, she reapplied her favorite lip gloss, washed her hands, and walked out the door. Messing with her clutch she was not paying attention to where she was walking and ran straight into something.

Well, that something was actually a man and that man was none other than Drake Jameson. She said sorry about 1,000 times and asked if he was okay.

He laughed and said, "Yes, Mel, I'm fine. Are you okay?"

She said, "Yes" and that she was sorry again and he looked at her and said, "Mel, I really am fine, I promise."

Then he leaned in towards her almost like he was going to kiss her. She could not believe this. Was Drake Jameson actually trying to kiss her? She had forgotten how strong that feeling was and grabbed his arm to keep from falling. He ran his hand through her hair and soon her back was up against the wall and she was kissing him back harder and harder.

She could not remember the last time she had kissed someone with such ferocity. Except maybe that tequila night when Drake kissed her, but that was old news. Why did she suddenly feel like her stomach was full of butterflies? Was it just from the alcohol or was it kissing Drake Jameson? She told herself, that kiss, the tequila night, was years ago.

So many things had changed and according to Facebook he was clearly not single. *Wait, neither am I*, she thought. *What am I doing?*

She tried to tell her brain to stop analyzing every little detail and just enjoy this moment. It worked for a little while, but when she finally opened her eyes, she was staring straight at an open-mouthed Kate.

She made a beeline for the bathroom and after Melanie finally convinced Drake to stop kissing her, she darted in after her. She made sure they were alone and then before she could say anything, Kate interjected.

"OMG! You were kissing Drake! I mean Drake was kissing you! Does this mean we will finally be sisters-in-law? It is about damn time! Do you still like him? What are you going to do? Can I call Tiffani and tell her! This is so unbelievably awesome! I mean really, it is about damn time. You guys should've been together for years by now!"

Melanie interrupted her, shaking her head and saying, "Kate, nothing is going to happen. Drake is with Tiffani and I am with Clayton. Do not say a word. Just act like you never saw anything. Pinky promise?"

Kate looked at her pleading to allow her to at least tell Daniel. Melanie said, "Absolutely not, especially not him."

Pretty soon there was a knock at the door and Daniel said, "Hey girls, the limo is here. Are you ready to go?" Melanie gave Kate a look and the girls stumbled out the door, practically falling into the limo. Back in her room, in her own king size bed, Melanie could not stop thinking about that kiss. *What if Drake Jameson really was her soul mate? Could they really be meant for each other even this many years later? What if he was the one she was supposed to be with? Could you make a mistake and really miss your fate?*

Chapter 17

Melanie fell asleep and slept until 11:00 when her cell phone woke her up. Kate groggily said to be ready for lunch at 1:00 and hung up. Clearly the beautiful bride was not feeling too great this morning.

She had to force herself to get out of the plush, cloudlike bed and into the shower. As she swallowed three Ibuprofen, between gulps of Gatorade, she kept thinking about the kiss. She replayed the kiss over and over as she washed her hair, shaved her legs, dried her hair, and put on her make-up.

As she was dusting bronzer over her already tanned skin, she shook her head and said aloud, "This is silly. Drake Jameson is practically engaged. Nothing is going to come of this."

She was embarrassed of how childish she was being. She was almost twenty-eight years old and was acting no different than a thirteen-year-old with a crush.

She just wished she could call and tell someone, but who could she tell and what good would that do.

Normally she would call her sister, Madison, but she always felt like she was bothering her lately. Madison was working on her residency. After finishing nursing school early, the "brainiac" in her family just couldn't be finished with school. She was going to be a neonatologist and it fit her perfectly because she loved babies.

Her little sister was not so little, but the more she thought about it, the more she realized her little sister had been more like her big sister for years. Madison always knew what she wanted. If she set her mind on something, she didn't stop until she made it happen. Melanie had been the lost one.

Melanie thought journalism and advertising was her career path. After losing Ryan, she thought for a while about being a substance abuse counselor. She didn't want anyone else to feel responsible the way she did.

When the first therapist didn't help, she tried another one. It was through therapy that she learned to let go of her guilt. She knew that Ryan was not the one for her. No matter how much she fantasized and romanticized their love story in her mind. It was apparent that he had a drinking problem way before he ever tried the cocaine.

No matter what she would have done, he would have always chosen drinking over her and their relationship. It was a constant fight when he was drinking and he was always full of excuses. She was lucky she still had friends who supported her. She thought about calling her friend Sydney. She had always been supportive, but she didn't know how she would react to the Drake situation. Four years ago, she would have thought it was "amazing and just like a movie." In fact, those were her words when she told her about their hookup four years ago. Now though, Sydney would probably tell her to grow up already and quit dreaming about Drake Jameson.

Anyone else would think badly of her because if she wanted to admit it or not, she had cheated on Clayton and she knew he was too nice of a guy for that. She glanced at the clock and hurriedly tried to find something to wear.

Chapter 18

I know I need to break things off with Clayton, she thought to herself.

He's just so nice and deserves someone who really wants to be with him. I know I am not that person. Thinking these thoughts in her head as she dug through her suitcase, she made the decision to end things when she returned to Florida.

She kept thinking these thoughts as she got dressed. Grabbing her sunglasses, she met the girls in the lobby. It was obvious Melanie and Holli were the only ones really feeling up for a day of shopping, but Kate, the other bridesmaids, Patty, Kate's mother, and Veronica Jameson were joining them for lunch at the Seasons Lounge at the Four Seasons Hotel. Veronica gave Melanie a big hug and she forgot how much she had missed the Jameson family. Patty asked how the bachelorette party went and then glanced at Kate still wearing her sunglasses in the restaurant and clearly not wanting to be anywhere but in bed, said, "Well, I guess it was a good time then?" Holli nodded her head yes and the other girls agreed.

Melanie enjoyed her lunch while centerpieces and bouquets were discussed. After the plates were cleared, the ladies ventured back to the hotel while Holli and Melanie visited Michigan Avenue. Melanie loved to shop, but just didn't have the extra money lately. Still, she had to check out Michigan Avenue.

Holli bought bags worth of things, but Melanie only window shopped. After less than two hours of browsing Michigan Avenue, both girls decided they wanted to take a nap before the rehearsal at six.

After pushing snooze on her alarm several times, she decided against showering for the second time that day and just focused on getting ready.

Her lilac, satin cocktail dress fit her in all the right places. It made her legs look miles long, but yet toned, and her whole body was glowing from the year-round Florida sun. She added some black T-Strap heels and some black and silver hoops. At the church, Kate was playing dictator and ordering the bridesmaids to one side and the groomsmen to another.

Holli was pleasantly surprised to be paired up with Ben from the night before and Melanie found herself being walked down the aisle by none other than Drake Jameson.

She shot Kate an "I can't believe you" look and hoped he wouldn't say anything about the kiss last night. Maybe he didn't even remember last night. After all, they had all been drinking quite a lot. She was just going to pretend like nothing happened and that it wasn't weird to be walking down the aisle with him. She put on her best game face and marched on. She tried to imagine how enchanting the church would look tomorrow with hundreds of flowers being flown in for the occasion.

When she found her place at the front of the church, Drake squeezed her hand and winked at her. She could not believe this, *what is he doing?* she thought.

He has some nerve. Where is his girlfriend? she wanted to say. Then she realized one person that was missing from this weekend. Where was Tiffani? Shouldn't she be here by now? Maybe they really had broken up and maybe he really did want to be with her. It could happen, right? After all, she sure was due for some happiness sometime in her life. After practicing for over an hour and a half, Kate was finally satisfied and it was time for dinner. The rehearsal dinner was at an upscale Italian restaurant and Melanie loved it. Everything was delicious and as she was enjoying her third glass of wine, Drake came and sat by her.

Chapter 19

After an awkward silence, she finally asked the first thing she could think of, "So, how was your dinner?"

He just laughed and said, "It was great. How was yours?"

She nodded her head yes and took another sip of her wine.

He looked at her glass and said, "Well, Mel, you are growing up. Did you trade in your beer for wine?"

She just laughed and said, "Oh, I still love my beer, just thought wine went better with this dress."

He laughed and told her that was a smart decision because she'd never looked better. With her face blushing red, he left and she was left wondering. *Where was Tiffani? Was she even coming at all?*

She really wished she could talk to someone and wished her parents were coming tonight instead of tomorrow. Her dad thought it was a better idea to drive in the morning, so they were coming before noon tomorrow. She sipped her wine as Kate and Daniel thanked everyone for being there and for sharing their special day. Then they told the bridal party not to drink too much tonight and to be ready for pictures by 2:00.

The girls were going to Ruby Room Salon and Spa to get facials and to have their hair and nails done. They were to be ready in the lobby at 11:00. Since the wedding wasn't until 5:00, Melanie was anticipating a long day. She was going to her room to call Clayton and go to bed when she felt a hand on her shoulder. She turned around and was suddenly staring into green eyes.

Drake said, "Hey, Mel, want to grab a drink with me in the bar?"

She nodded her head yes and followed him into the bar, the whole time thinking, *what am I doing?* She ordered a "Pomtini" and sipped it slowly as he drank a Coors Light.

He laughed and asked her what had happened to "his beer girl." She couldn't believe it. "His beer girl?" Since when had she ever been anything of his? She just laughed and said, "Maybe later."

And he smiled and said, "I sure hope so." Ben and Holli joined them for a while and pretty soon one "Pomtini" turned into two. Then they were alone.

He asked her about Florida, law school and, surprisingly, her dating situation. She told him Florida was amazing, that he should visit and that law school was ridiculously hard, but she was glad she had stuck it out. She said that she was dating someone and that he wasn't coming because he had to work.

He told her about life in their hometown, about who was getting married, and who was still around. He told her about his frequent business trips to Japan and how the business was growing. They talked and talked and she couldn't help but think how right it felt to be sitting next to him again.

She ordered a Bud Light and they reminisced and told stories about when they were little. They kept interrupting each other to tell the ending of the story and they were both laughing and talking about the good old days. Pretty soon the bartender told them that it was almost 1:00 and the bar was closing.

She knew she should have been in bed hours ago so when Drake asked if she wanted to go somewhere else, she said, "I better not. I have to be in tip top condition tomorrow and a lot earlier than you, lucky duck."

He said he understood and surprisingly walked her to her hotel room. When he got to the door, she gave him a hug, but instead of hugging her back he kissed her again. The feelings she felt last night came rushing back and she found herself kissing him back. She wanted to invite him into her room. After all who would ever know? But then she remembered how he acted four years ago and decided against it.

She kissed him on the cheek and hugged him again before going into her room. She saw her cell phone sitting on the dresser and realized she had forgotten it all night. She had seven missed calls.

Three from her mom, one from her dad, one from Kali, and two from Clayton. She decided it was too late to call her mom or dad back and called Clayton. He asked about dinner and said he just wanted to check in with his gorgeous girl.

She told him she was great and that the dinner was amazing and that she was having fun. He asked if she missed him. Not wanting to hurt his feelings she lied and said, "Yes." She thought to herself, *I know I am not being fair to him. I have to talk to him as soon as I get back.* Then fell asleep dreaming of Drake.

Chapter 20

Her time at the spa was very relaxing and she truly enjoyed her massage, but she could not stop thinking about her time with Drake. She wondered if maybe this time things would actually work out. After all, they were much older and more mature. When all the girls' fingers and toes were polished and their faces fresh and glowing, Kate told them it was time to go back to the hotel to get ready. Melanie knew her parents would be here soon and she stopped at the lobby to see if they had already checked in. They had.

While waiting for the elevator, a girl joined her. She paid no attention, but soon realized it was Drake's on-again-off-again girlfriend, Tiffani. She almost didn't recognize her. Gone was her blonde shoulder length hair, replacing it was long, sleek black, curly hair. The only thing she recognized were her piercing blue eyes. She said, "Hello," and Tiffani said the same. They were not enemies, just not really friends. They had only met a few times and the last time Tiffani was too drunk to remember meeting her. The elevator doors opened and both girls pushed their floor number. Suddenly, something shiny caught Melanie's eye. Tiffani was wearing a huge diamond ring and it was on her LEFT hand!

Why was Tiffani wearing a diamond ring? Why was she here? she screamed in her mind.

Drake told me they broke up! Did he lie to me? She felt like such a fool. How could she have believed everything would be okay? Nothing had changed at all. Melanie felt like crying, but kept it together long enough for Tiffani to get off the elevator, and on Drake's floor at that.

Chapter 21

Alone in the elevator, Melanie felt so foolish. Tears were falling and she realized she felt the same way four years ago. She could still remember her conversation with Kate.

She couldn't believe she let herself think she actually had a future with Drake Jameson. She had called Kate for some perspective. Kate had been aware of Melanie's newly discovered feelings and was hoping Drake felt the same way.

"Kate, I don't even know if I would consider him a friend right now. I mean I put myself out there and I feel so, so stupid. A friend wouldn't let another friend feel like this."

"I'm sorry Mel. I really thought something was going to come of this, but Daniel said, 'He's talking to Tiffani again.' I'm sorry. I just found out. Otherwise, I would have told you sooner. I promise."

"He is? Since when?"

"I guess she showed up at the airport when he was coming home from Japan. I didn't know any of this. No one did. Daniel just found out too."

"Relax. I'm not mad at you. I just want to get my facts straight. So, he has been talking to her this whole time?"

"I guess so. That's all I know. She was at the airport and he's been to see her a few times. He's leaving again this week though. Maybe you should just show up at his house and tell him how you really feel?"

"Kate, no. He knows how I feel and he obviously does not care. God, I feel so incredibly stupid right now."

"Don't say that. I am sorry. He's just a guy and they don't know what they want sometimes."

"No, Kate. He obviously does. He wants Tiffani and he's probably been with her this whole time."

"I don't know. I am sorry. I just. I am sorry. Are you okay?"

"Yeah, I'll be fine. Just glad you told me before I made myself look even dumber."

She could not believe she almost fell for Drake again.

He is certainly not single! In fact, he is engaged! She wanted to scream at him.

She wiped her tears and tried to pull herself together. She did not want her mom and dad to know she had been crying. She knocked on their door and her mom answered the door.

She hugged her asking, "Hi, honey. How has the weekend been so far?"

Melanie couldn't help but notice her mom was acting as if she was hiding something.

She hugged her dad and then her mom said, "Why don't you go next door and see who's there?"

Melanie was instantly excited. She thought her sister Madison had changed her mind and made the trip. The door opened. Suddenly she was enveloped in a big strong hug. It was Clayton, not Madison.

He said, "Hi, pretty girl. Did you think I'd let you go to the wedding alone?"

She couldn't believe he was here. "What are you doing here? How did you get off work?"

He said, "I couldn't miss seeing you in your pretty dress, so I moved some of my appointments and left early this morning. Your parents picked me up at the airport on their way to the hotel."

She was suddenly very happy to see him and hugged him tighter. She thought, *Seriously, he is just such a good guy.* She started to second guess her decision to break things off. She remembered how patient and understanding he had been with her. He was the one who helped to heal her broken heart.

Before Clayton, she was in love with a fantasy. One that died and one that never began. Clayton was real. He cared about her. He didn't lie.

He showed up when she didn't even know she needed him. He taught her to trust and showed her that there really were nice guys. Nice guys who didn't just like her when it was convenient for them. Or when they had too much to drink.

Thinking about it, she realized most of her encounters with Drake had been when she was drinking. Her worst times with Ryan were when they were drinking. Her life with Clayton was an honest, adult relationship. It wasn't just someone to make out with when she was drunk and silly.

He was someone who asked about her day, who cared about her opinion. He wanted to make her happy. He had been her rock, the only support she had in her new life in Florida. *Am I really going to throw that away?*

100

Drake means nothing to me. Even though that kiss had been spectacular, she thought to herself.

What is it about Drake Jameson? Why does he make me feel like that? It has to be the alcohol. Maybe I was wrong about Clayton. Maybe this is where I should be. Clayton makes me feel so safe and he is always there for me. Even if I don't deserve him.

Chapter 22

Drake

Drake could not believe Tiffani was here. *What is she doing?* Sure, she was invited months ago, but that was before he ended things. He couldn't deal with her and her drama anymore. He asked Daniel and Kate to tell her she was uninvited, but they said they didn't want to be in the middle of anything. *Who does she think she is? She just waltzed her way up to my room acting like nothing ever happened.*

He wanted her to go away. He wanted to tell her to leave right now, but the wedding was starting. He couldn't deal with this today of all days. He had to give a speech soon and he could feel his nerves. He hated public speaking. He had asked his dad to just give a speech for everyone. He knew he was best man and that it was an honor. *I just can't deal with this right now.*

He didn't want Tiffani to ruin Daniel and Kate's special night. He wished he could just go talk to Melanie. He was worried if she knew Tiffani was here. *What if she thinks I invited her?*

He also knew if anyone could help him not feel so nervous, it would be Melanie. *Too bad there isn't time for that.* He was thankful the wedding party had to take pictures before the ceremony. He would take any excuse to stay away from Tiffani.

Just as he was thinking of a reason to get out of this hotel room, there was a knock at the door.

Chapter 23

Melanie put Drake out of her mind and kissed Clayton before meeting Kate and the girls to get dressed. Her dress looked amazing with her tousled, half-up do. Kate had a makeup artist do each girl's makeup. When the artist was finished, Melanie was pleasantly surprised. She examined the handiwork in the mirror and thought she looked so glamorous.

Soon the bridesmaids were finished and when Kate's turn was through, Veronica came and told them it was time for pictures. Melanie would not look at Drake the whole time the photographer took the wedding party's pictures. Or when they had to walk down the aisle together. Or during the entire ceremony.

He kept trying to get her attention, but she refused to look into those green hypnotic eyes again. The ceremony was beautiful. The church was filled with cream and dark red roses. Kate and Daniel said their vows and she couldn't help but have tears in her eyes. It was a picture-perfect ceremony. She couldn't imagine less, seeing as how Veronica Jameson was a part of the picture. She certainly had a knack for decorating and an eye for detail. Not one flower was out of place.

After a few more hundred pictures, the wedding party hopped into a white stretch Hummer Limo and headed back to hotel for the reception.

The food was amazing: lobster tail, filet mignon, shrimp cocktail; there was so much to choose from. As the guests were served, it was time for the wedding toasts. Drake's was very heartfelt and he told embarrassing stories about Daniel and him growing up.

Then he said how he hoped to find someone who made him as happy as Kate made Daniel.

Melanie could not help but be bitter, thinking, *You already have that 'stupid,' apparently with Tiffani.* She tried her best to be pleasant and smiled and clapped through clenched teeth. She sat with the bridal party and then as soon as she was finished eating, she went to sit by Clayton. She was listening to him talk about his weekend when an announcement was made that the bridal party needed to be on the dance floor.

Just her luck, she had to dance with Drake. After an awkward dance, she walked away and danced with the other bridesmaids.

She danced one dance with Daniel. "I'm just so happy for you and Kate," she told him. The rest of the night she danced with Clayton. Fast or slow, he was a great date and she was having such a great time.

Suddenly she felt a hand on her shoulder and Drake was asking Clayton if he could dance with her for old times' sake.

Before she could answer, Clayton said, "Of course, be my guest."

Just like Clayton to be a gentleman, she thought to herself. He was not the jealous type. He knew Melanie and the Jamesons had been friends since they were in diapers. Melanie could not believe Drake had the guts to even ask her to dance. She wouldn't even look at him.

He has to know I am mad. What kind of guy kisses someone when they clearly have a fiancée? she screeched in her mind.

Once again, Melanie misjudged someone's character. The more she thought about it, the more she couldn't wait to get back to her life in Florida. In the beginning, she was scared to move so far away from everything she ever knew. Now, she realized that was the appeal.

Florida was thousands of miles away from anything familiar. She never had to worry about running into people or places of her past and she never had to worry about seeing Drake Jameson. Plus, she loved the sunshine, she loved being by the beach and she loved her job. When she decided to study law, it made sense. The law was black or white. There was no gray area. You were either guilty or innocent. There is no in between. She wished her life was more like that; either you made the right choice, or you made the wrong choice.

Chapter 24

Drake

Obviously, he knew Melanie was upset with him. He figured it had to do with Tiffani, but he didn't know for sure. He saw her kissing her boyfriend before the ceremony and was instantly pissed. She acted like they weren't even serious, but clearly, they were. He watched them dancing and couldn't stand it any longer. He asked Melanie to dance to see if she would talk to him. He kept asking her what was wrong. He knew from the look on her face, it was Tiffani.

He tried to explain, "I swear we are not together. She just showed up here." Melanie just rolled her eyes.

He knew she didn't believe him. *Why should she? I lied about Tiffani in the past, but this time it was different.*

"Mel, I promise. We are really finished. I told her not to come, but she wouldn't listen. Besides, what's Clay or whatever doing here?"

Melanie looked sad. She asked, "If you're telling the truth then why is she wearing a ring?"

He didn't know why they were wasting such a special moment talking about Tiffani. He just wanted her to leave. He didn't want to be surrounded by all of these people when he was trying to say something so important.

He didn't know what to say or how to explain any of it. He just knew that he couldn't lose her again.

He said, "Mel, seriously, meet me outside on the rooftop and let's really talk. Tell Clay you have to go do some bridesmaid thing or something and come talk to me. Please? There is so much I need to tell you and I can't do it here. Not with my parents and all of these people around. Please just meet me later and trust me." She didn't look so angry anymore and they actually danced for about a minute before the song was over.

He was secretly hoping that she would meet him later and that he could finally explain. If she didn't, then he was going to follow her to the airport. No matter what, Melanie Dickson was not leaving this weekend until he told her how he really felt. His thoughts were interrupted when he felt a tapping on his shoulder. He knew from the claw-like nails, it was Tiffani. He just wanted her to leave, but she wasn't taking the hint. He was afraid she would cause a scene, so he convinced her to go outside with him.

Chapter 25
Melanie

Drake kept trying to explain. While thoughts raced through her mind, *I'm not going to listen to his lies anymore. I may have fallen for him in the past, but not again.* She stared at him incredulously, "Do you think I am stupid? Am I really supposed to believe you? She is wearing a diamond ring, Drake! By the way his name is Clayton and he is more of a man than you will ever be."

She was proud. She finally stood up for herself. She even tried to walk off, but Drake wouldn't let her. He grabbed her hands and said, "Mel, listen. I am telling you the truth. I have nothing to do with Tiffani. I didn't give her a stupid ring. I am never going to give her a ring. She's not the one for me. I've known it for a long time."

Melanie just shook her head as he pleaded, "You have got to believe me. I promise I am telling you the truth."

He asked her to meet him later on the rooftop when he could explain things better.

"I just don't know what I believe right now."

Drake kept pleading, "Please just talk to me. I need to talk to you." She wanted to believe him. She just didn't know if he was telling the truth.

She didn't have much time to think. Tiffani interrupted them. She did not look happy. Not in the slightest.

Chapter 26

Seeing Tiffani so angry, Melanie didn't know what to think. *Is she mad because Drake was talking to me? Or is she mad because Drake doesn't want to be with her anymore?* Melanie wanted to believe Drake with all of her heart. She knew deep down he wasn't a bad guy. They both made mistakes, and the timing had never been right.

Thinking back, had either of them ever been single at the same time? Other than the hookup when she had practically thrown herself at him in the hot tub? She thought about that night and she was embarrassed.

She was not the kind of girl to chase after a guy. What was it about Drake Jameson that made her just completely lose her control? Sitting at the table with Clayton, she kept thinking. She kept trying to tell herself that *Clayton is who she should be with. Kissing Drake is a mistake. He doesn't want to be with me and I need to just accept that.* Even though she couldn't stop thinking about the kiss the night before. *It's not love, it's just the circumstances.*

They were at an amazingly beautiful wedding. They were old friends. That was it. Of course, it would feel romantic. They had a very long history. *The past is the past, Drake is my past, Clayton is my future; that is how it is.*

Still, she couldn't help but wonder what he wanted to tell her. Or why he wanted her to meet him on the rooftop later.

Clayton grabbed her by the hand and said, "Gorgeous, can I talk to you outside for a while?"

She said yes and followed him all the while thinking, "Why does he want to go outside? It's Chicago, it's April and it's quite cold." As if reading her mind, he offered her his suit jacket and put his arm around her. Outside they realized they were not alone, Drake and Tiffani were outside too, only they were arguing. Drake was standing with his arms crossed and Tiffani was crying. She was pleading with him as he put her into a cab. He walked towards a bench as the car drove off, Clayton said, "Mel, go talk to him. He looks like he could use a friend. I am going to run upstairs to get something from the room. I'll be right back."

Chapter 27

Melanie sat down next to Drake.

"So, what happened?"

"Nothing new."

"What do you mean?"

"I told her we were over for good this time. I told her she knew that and she never should have showed up. We aren't getting back together ever again and if she wanted to be friends, I could try to do that, but nothing else. She got really upset and started crying. She said, 'She was sorry. She doesn't know why she cheats on me, because she loves me and she wants to be with me.' I don't even care about the cheating. It never really felt like cheating, because I've never even been in love with her. I can't love her. I can't love anyone, because I've been in love with the same person since I was eight years old. I just never knew how to say it and I was too stupid to realize it until she loved someone else."

Melanie felt like all of the air had been sucked out of her lungs. She felt like she was dreaming, but she knew she was clearly awake. Drake Jameson was telling her everything she had hoped and prayed he would say for years.

He grabbed her hand and said, "Melanie, I have loved you since I was eight years old, even though I know I haven't always acted like it. I was an idiot. Being with Tiffani was just comfortable. After a while you get to a certain point where you don't want to go look for someone else. I knew I loved you when we were in the hot tub. I knew I loved you when I kissed you after the shot of tequila. I just didn't want to settle down yet. You're the only person I've ever loved. I just never told you and then it was too late. I don't care anymore. I can't pretend that I don't love you. Every time I see you, it's like these old feelings just come rushing back. If you want to be with Clay or whatever then that is fine, but I can't sit here and not tell you how I feel. I just always thought we would end up together, but I messed up. I never called you. I never told you how special you are to me. I kept hoping that you would come back to town after law school, but I know now that you won't. I can't do anything to change your mind, but tell you that I love you and I always have."

"Mel, this weekend made me realize that you are the only girl for me. You have always been there no matter what. No one makes me feel the way you do. I feel like I'm eight years old around you. I laugh more with you than with anyone else and I have so much fun with you."

Melanie was speechless. Was she dreaming? Was Drake Jameson actually saying what she'd been wishing for so many years? Suddenly he grabbed her in his arms and kissed her. This kiss surpassed last night's and all the other nights before. She knew it sounded cliché but she actually felt like there was electricity between them.

When she finally opened her eyes, she was staring at an open-mouthed Clayton. He was holding a bouquet of stargazer lilies, her favorite flowers. She didn't know if she should stay with Drake or run after him. She tried to follow him into the elevator, but he shut the doors on her. Standing there waiting for another elevator's door to open, she dug her hands into the pockets of his jacket.

As the tears rolled down her face, she felt something soft in her hand. She pulled out a velvet box and in between tears she opened it. Inside was a diamond ring. Suddenly it all made sense. She thought to herself, *That's why Clayton came this weekend. He wanted to propose. What should I do? I never wanted to hurt Clayton. He is never anything but nice to me. He is a good man. How did I make such a mess of things?*

Drake Jameson was just a dream she had when she was little and had never stopped dreaming, but Clayton was the real thing. Except, now Drake isn't a dream.

Trying to sort out the situation in her mind, she thought, *What should I do? Should I listen to Drake? Or should I try and find Clayton and apologize?*

Chapter 28

Drake

He did it! He told Melanie how he really felt. He couldn't believe it. It had only taken him 20 years, but he told her he loved her. He even apologized for all of the times he was an ass. Then he kissed her. It was the perfect moment and then it was over. Melanie jerked away from him and was chasing something. When he turned around, he saw her boyfriend, Clayton, holding flowers and walking into an empty elevator with his head down.

Shit, he thought. *He saw us.*

He knew how it felt to see your girlfriend kissing someone else. He didn't want to hurt him like that, but he just couldn't let Mel leave without telling her how he felt. He planned to tell her everything later on the rooftop if she would have just met him like he asked. Why did Tiffani have to make such a scene? He could have told Mel later. He just wanted to be alone with her, but now wasn't the right time. Or was it? Is there ever really a perfect time to say something so important? No, he blew it. He had four years to tell her. Why did he wait until now, at his brother's wedding of all places? He didn't know if he should run after her or if she would come back. What if she didn't choose him? What if he really was too late? He just knew that he had finally told her how he felt, even if it wasn't the "perfect" time.

Chapter 29

Melanie ran after Clayton trying to explain. He didn't want to hear any excuses.

"I think this is probably for the best. You clearly have feelings for Drake."

"No, I don't. I don't know what that was."

"Melanie, then what was that kiss? Do you love me? Do you want to be with me?"

"I just don't know what I want right now."

"Then, that right there is your answer."

He told her that it was all for the best, because clearly, she had feelings for Drake. She couldn't deny her feelings, so she just didn't say anything. She gave him his jacket back, never mentioning what she had found in the pocket. The next morning, he flew back to Florida alone. Her family was shocked to hear he left. They were expecting an announcement. She never explained exactly what happened, but they eventually figured it out. She stayed in the city until her flight left later that night. She spent most of the day exploring the city. She walked the streets alone with her thoughts. She knew she had to talk things over with Clayton. She texted him asking to meet her for coffee the next day.

Surprisingly, he responded and agreed to meet. On her flight home she tried to sort out her feelings and figure out what to say.

Walking into the coffee shop, her hair in a messy bun, wearing leggings and a t-shirt, she knew she looked like she hadn't slept much. Her flight was running behind. When the Uber finally dropped her off, it was after midnight. She didn't even unpack. She was emotionally and physically drained from the busy weekend.

Feeling nervous but thankful he agreed to meet, she quickly ordered her drink and spotted him at a nearby table.

Gripping her coffee cup helped to calm her nerves. She sat down across from him and held her breath as he started to talk.

"I never knew Drake was anything but a friend to you."

"He is. I don't know what that kiss was about."

"It looked like you were definitely more than friends. You looked happy."

Melanie didn't say anything. She couldn't explain what happened.

"I was going to propose. I had a plan. I flew there to surprise you, to tell you that I wanted to start a life together."

"I know."

"What do you mean you know?"

"I found the ring in the pocket."

"You did?"

"I can't marry you though."

"Because of Drake?"

"No, because we aren't in love."

"Well, being with you makes me happy. I thought we had something great together."

"It was pretty great. You're a wonderful guy. You're just not the right one for me."

"What does that even mean? Do you even know what you want, Melanie? I've sat by and been patient. I tried to understand how hard it was to move on from Ryan, but I don't think you even know what you want."

"I don't think I do either. I just know that we don't love each other. Someday, you will find some wonderful woman who will love you exactly as you deserve. I am just not that person."

"How do you know?"

"Because love isn't something you try to talk yourself into. It's something you can't explain."

"You promise you're happy?"

"I think I will be. I know we both will be."

He hugged her goodbye and told her, "Good luck with the bar exam."

They ended things much like their relationship, mature. She didn't mean to hurt him and he understood that. They didn't end badly. She didn't fall apart. No one died. She was focused on something more important – passing the bar exam. She worked too hard in law school not to give it her all.

After Ryan died, her mom helped her decide what to do with her life. Her parents let her live with them for free, while she studied for the LSAT. They didn't even ask her to get a job. Her dad was thrilled with her choice to study law. He said he always dreamed she would become a lawyer. She only started making slogans and advertisements for the gym by accident. She was just at the gym one day, probably trying to run into Drake, when the owner was complaining about the lack of marketing. She gave her a few ideas and the owner loved them. It was a great way to earn a little money and didn't take away from her studying. The LSAT was hard and she was worried she blew it. She was more than pleased with her results and took it as a sign that things were only going to get better.

Her parents didn't agree with her applying to out-of-state schools. They worried about her and wanted to make sure she was safe. Melanie explained to them that she needed to do this for herself. Her mom was supportive and always encouraged her to do what made her happy. They had helped her find her apartment in Florida and visited as much as they could. Melanie knows her mom was just happy she was not hiding in her childhood bedroom anymore.

Law school gave her a purpose. It helped put the fire back into her. She couldn't just give up now and for what? Maybe a relationship with Drake? No, she worked too hard to do that. No boy was ever going to have that kind of control in her life again.

After the wedding, Drake had called her wanting to talk more. She told him she needed to take some time to think. Drake wasn't a patient person though. She knew that. Barely a day went by without a text from him saying, "Hi" or "How are you?" She was always nice, but she didn't want to just jump into the relationship. What if it wasn't what she wanted? What if it was one big disappointment? It was a huge decision. It's not like they would just casually date.

If she chose Drake, then she was saying goodbye to everything she worked so hard to rebuild. She had a new life in Florida and her world did not revolve around Drake Jameson.

She focused all of her energy on studying. She joined a study group with some of the students she had had classes with. The study group helped keep her accountable and kept her focused. Plus, it was nice to get to know people outside of class. She quickly made friends with Stella. They shared a common love for Starbucks Caramel Macchiatos. The next time the study group met, Stella brought her one as well.

In her free time, she hung out with some girls in her study group. She tried paddleboard yoga. When her new friend Stella suggested it, she said, "Absolutely no way!"

"You have to try it first."

"Being on a flimsy board in the water. Are you crazy? This is Florida, there aren't just fish, there are alligators in this water."

"There are no alligators, I promise. It's fun. It sure beats studying."

"You have a point there. Okay, I'll think about it."

Melanie had tried yoga in the past and it really helped her calm down. Between her grueling study schedule and trying to decide what to do about Drake, her nerves were pretty shot. Anything calming would be welcomed.

She told Stella she would join her for the next class.

The instructor informed them, it's okay to fall in. In fact, it is pretty "refreshing."

He also assured them, "There are no alligators in this part of the bay."

Melanie could instantly feel herself start to relax. Finding her *drishti* at the end of her board, she kept her balance as she wobbled into tree pose. Balancing on one foot on land is difficult, but balancing on one foot on a wobbly board was almost impossible. Still, she stayed dry and solid on the board. *I did it!* she thought to herself. She was so proud of herself and hardly thought about the fish that were most likely swimming beneath her.

As she rested in *Savasana* pose, she realized her mind hadn't wandered. She didn't think about Drake, or civil procedure, or contracts, or torts the whole time she was on the water.

She thanked Stella for inviting her, making the yoga class a new part of her routine. As the test date crept closer, she felt determined and ready. Yoga increased her confidence and helped her focus. Her study group kept her on track.

The morning of the test, she made sure to eat breakfast. She tried not to pay attention to her phone as she got ready, but several Good Luck messages flashed on her screen.

Four long hours later, she was finished. She thought to herself, *I did it!*

She knew she had studied and prepared as best as she could. Sure, she had impending fear that she bombed it. Drowning her fears in Bloody Marys with Stella and a few other girls from the study group was the best way to cope. Deep down, though, she thought, *I gave it my best.* She wasn't distracted by a new relationship. Her dream was important and she was sticking to the plan. The girl she lost six years ago was back and she was proud of herself for getting to this point.

Six long weeks later, reading her results with Stella, she was thrilled to know she passed. The study group celebrated with champagne.

Waking up groggily to someone knocking on her apartment door, she was surprised to see flowers being delivered.

Expecting them to be from her family, she was surprised to read, "Congratulations! I always believed in you! You will be the best lawyer." The from line was signed by Drake.

She wondered "How did he know?" She had only told her family and a few friends from home. Oh, and Kate. *Good old Kate*, she thought. She always kept Melanie updated on Drake. Apparently, she was keeping Drake updated on Melanie as well.

Happy for the flowers and realizing she owed Drake a phone call at least. *Who knows if he will even answer? I've been down this road before,* she thought to herself. She remembered when she had called him, excited after taking the LSAT. He didn't answer and never phoned her back.

As she found his name in her phone, she thought, *What do I have to lose?*

The bar exam was over. Her nights of studying were gone. She had new found freedom. Surprisingly, he answered on the first ring.

"How are you? How's Florida?"

"Great. How are you?"

"Good! Things have been busy at work. So, tell me how was the Bar?"

She told him all about the grueling exam and her new love of paddleboard yoga.

He laughed, "I just can't believe that you would choose to do anything in fish-filled water."

She just laughed and said, "Hey, I'm not afraid of fish anymore!"

He said, "Oh yeah, well I guess there's a lot of things I don't know about you then."

She laughed and said, "It was really fun. I am glad I tried something new."

He said, "I am, too. You sound really happy, like really, really happy."

She said, "I know. I am."

Their phone calls became a nightly routine and she looked forward to telling him about her day. She enjoyed his stories of working in the family factory. Laughing when he told her how he tried to fix a conveyor belt while boxes were flying off the shelves. He never pressured her or asked her to make a decision. A few months later, a plane ticket home arrived. *I know I need to see him to decide how I really feel,* she thought as she booked the flight. She planned to spend some time with her family and then casually let him know she was in town.

Stepping off the plane, distracted with her carry-on bag, she looked up to familiar green eyes.

Drake stood by the gate, holding flowers. *I should have known,* she thought.

Hugging her, she thanked him for the flowers and for driving her. She was surprised, but she should have known when she used the ticket he sent. The drive to their hometown took some time. They laughed and joked and she sang along with the radio. Then Drake said, "Mel, my feelings haven't changed. I love talking to you every night."

"I know. Me, too. I just don't know what I want to do right now."

"I'll go slow if that's what you want. Just try and give us a chance."

When he dropped her off at home, her mom acted surprised. Melanie knew Drake told her he was the one picking her up. You can't just surprise people when the airport is more than an hour away.

Her visit home was spent mostly with her family. Madison was thrilled to see her. As she was asking about Drake, he texted asking her to dinner.

Chapter 30

Drake

After the wedding, Drake was trying not to bug Melanie too much. *I just don't know what she is going to do,* he thought to himself. He knew Clayton left alone the next morning, but that didn't mean anything.

He tried to give her some space. She said she needed time to think. "What does that even mean? Is that a few weeks, a few months? Hell, does she need another four years? What should I do?" he asked Kate.

"Just back off and don't rush her. Don't mess this up."

She knew what happened. She talked to Mel all of the time. He knew he had to do something. He wanted to get on a plane and go see her, but he figured that would freak her out.

When Kate told him she passed the bar exam, he thought, *That's my perfect excuse.* He sent congratulatory flowers instead. His heart was beating so fast when he picked up her call.

He was relieved when she thanked him for the flowers. He was worried she was going to be mad. *Like I am being pushy and can't take a hint.*

She thanked him for the flowers and asked, "What's new?"

Almost an hour later, he hung up the phone laughing. He kept picturing her trying to stay on a paddleboard and not thinking about what was in the water. *She sounded really happy. Maybe she worked things out with Clayton,* he worried to himself, with a pit in his stomach.

He wanted to ask her, but he was afraid of the answer. When their phone calls became a regular thing, he got bold and sent her a plane ticket home. He didn't want her to think he was being arrogant or trying to impress her.

I just want to show I care and I want to see her.

He thought about buying himself a ticket to Florida many times. He knew that wasn't the answer. *Plus, what would I do in Florida if she didn't want me there? I can't just show up without a plan.*

A few months later, he saw that she had booked her flight home. He knew he had to meet her at the airport. He didn't want to waste any more time or wait and see if she tried to meet up with him. It didn't matter that the airport was more than an hour away. He didn't tell her he was the one picking her up. He called Madison to tell her his plan. She didn't say much, just "Okay. Well, that's sure nice of you." Her reaction didn't do much to boost his confidence. Second guessing his decision as he made the drive, he checked her flight time again and tried to stay calm as he gripped the steering wheel. He followed the signs to ARRIVALS thinking to himself. *It's now or never. What's the worst that could happen?*

Epilogue

Melanie Jameson sat on the edge of the pool, her feet dangling into the crystal blue water. The sun was beginning to set and the steamy August air had begun to cool off. Her two-year-old daughter, Caroline, was squealing with joy as her daddy, Drake, threw her into the water. Melanie sipped lemonade as her bulging belly moved side to side. Her soon-to-be son seemed to be trying to kick his way out three months early. Caroline kept saying, "Watch me, Mommy! Watch me! I go so high!"

Sitting in the sun with her loving, growing family surrounding her, Melanie could not believe how happy she was. She had a beautiful daughter, a wonderful husband, and a soon-to-be son on the way. She was a lawyer at a well-known firm in her hometown. She practiced family law and it was so rewarding to help families through adoption. She also helped children find safe homes if their family members chose alcohol or drugs instead of being parents. She felt like she was making a difference in the world. She never lost her sense of focus and was living out her dreams.

She realized that she finally had her happily ever after. She knew that marrying Clayton would have been a mistake, just like staying with Ryan, even if he was sober and alive, would also be a mistake. Being with Ryan taught her what she didn't want in a relationship. Sure, it almost broke her and his death was awful, but she knew deep down that he was not the guy for her. Clayton was sweet, caring, dependable, and just plain nice, but he didn't give her butterflies. No matter how hard she tried to force it, she just wasn't in love with him.

After Drake met her at the airport, he made several visits to Florida. She flew home more frequently to visit as well. She spent time with her family and old friends, but she never made it home without seeing Drake. Every dinner, movie, even just a drive around town felt like no time had passed. She felt more like herself than ever before. It was hard to picture herself with anyone else. She knew he cared about her. He never pushed her to move home, but she knew his business wasn't going to move to Florida. They didn't date long. What was the point? They were both pushing thirty and there was no doubt they wanted to make this relationship work. When they told their parents they were dating, both of their families had been thrilled. Melanie's family more so, because it meant she would probably be moving home in the near future. They knew she was happy when she came to visit. At first, they thought it was because studying was finished.

Melanie's mom supported her. She also knew that Drake was a good guy and that he really cared about Melanie. She just wanted her daughter to be happy and she knew from her smile that she was. Her sister, Madison, had hugged her. She was so happy to hear the news and hopeful that Melanie would be moving home. She really missed her sister. Kate had screamed with happiness.

Daniel said, "You've always been like a sister. Now you really can be."

Her friend Sydney said, "About damn time you two figured it out!"

Drake's mom, Veronica, was the most excited.

She said, "I always knew this would happen. You kids have been crazy about each other your whole lives. Just last week, I found a box of your old love letters you wrote each other from summer camp. Do you remember that?"

It was strange how everyone seemed to know Drake and Melanie belonged together before they could figure it out. He proposed after only six months.

"I just can't wait any longer. I love you and only you. I always have and I always will. Will you marry me?"

Choking back tears, Melanie said, "Yes."

Drake and Melanie were married on the beaches of Mexico in a ceremony surrounded by only their family and friends. Veronica Jameson was not happy about the simplicity of the wedding. She was ecstatic about the romantic love story that spanned two decades. She was almost insistent on a grand affair. Melanie reminded her that Kate's wedding was not all that long ago.

Seeing as how Drake was the baby and had a way of convincing Veronica, she gave in and pretty much stayed out of the planning. It was really simple. The most extravagant item was Melanie's dress, which she stood her ground for. It was a mermaid fit with beading and lace covering the bodice and skirt. The bridesmaids wore short, lilac, strapless dresses and shoes were optional, seeing as how it was on the sandy beach. Melanie carried a bouquet of stargazer lilies and hibiscus and she and Drake wrote their own vows. Fireworks lit up the night sky as they promised to always love each other forever.

Love is scary. It can make you blind to reality, easy-to-forgive, and if you're with the wrong person, it can change you into someone you would not even recognize. But when you find the right person, love is wonderful. It can help you find everything you have been searching for. Her heart had and always would belong to Drake Jameson even if it had been a little beaten along the way. You can't fake feelings and you can't shake feelings. Mel knew that Drake really was her prince charming. He was the one that she should have been with all along.

CPSIA information can be obtained
at www.ICGtesting.com
Printed in the USA
LVHW010337210821
695735LV00011B/908